# FOREST RUNNERS

## WE THE MUTANTS
### BOOK 1

## Stella Fitzsimons

# Books by Stella Fitzsimons

## Mist Riders

*Luna*
*Winter*
*Silver Dust*
*Shadow Fall*
*Moonlight Mist*
*The Last Rider*

## We the Mutants

*Forest Runners*
*The Dark Legion*
*The Shadow Empire*
*Beyond the River of Time*
*Rise of the Saviors*
*We the Mutants Origins*

# FOREST RUNNERS

We the Mutants

FOREST RUNNERS



Cover Design by Get Covers



Published by Butterfly Electric Press

www.stellafitzsimons.com

*For Jiddu and Dylan,
now and forever.*

# Chapter 1

THE VISOR TIGHTENS AGAINST my face and the world goes black. Not the gentle dark of night where starlight and moonlight sneak through—no. This is absolute.

Good. They can't see me. Not yet.

My breath echoes in my ears as I step forward into the simulation with the virtual pulse gun steady in my grip. A faint, metallic buzz hangs in the air... false, synthetic. The ground feels soft and slick like wet clay.

My heart hammers against my ribs, a frantic drumbeat that echoes the distant, rhythmic thud of boots. The Sliman mutants are coming.

*We are a desperate, forbidden hope. We are a dark promise. We are legend. We are the Saviors.*

That's what we call ourselves anyway. The word feels hollow now, a childish boast in the face of evil. As if a handful of desperate kids could really save anything.

"Freya, the sequence!" Theo's voice crackles in my earpiece, yanking me from the shadows and back into the stifling confines of the simulator pod. "One plus one plus one! You need to move faster if you want to—"

"Yeah, I get it," I mutter. One plus one plus one doesn't equal three. It equals assault, hope and a knot in the stomach.

One, I yank down the lever to my left.

Two, I slam my palm on the big, pulsing red button in front of me.

Three, I check the flashing numbers on the goggle display, confirming the sequence.

One, two, three. Go time.

The simulated world explodes into my vision, filled with the nagging whine of energy weapons. I'm standing in the middle of Plantation-9, a dozen hostiles aiming at my avatar. Tactical pulse rifles glint under the harsh artificial sun, spitting bolts of blue energy. Shock bows hum with the tension of magnetic arrows. And then there is the KA-1 Plasmer with its ominous glow promising complete disintegration.

My fingers fumble for the shield activator. A wash of purple light envelops me just as the first shot strikes. The impact jolts through my virtual bones.

Another hit. And another. The shield flickers.

A warning display blinks in the corner of my visor: SHIELD AT 50%.

One more hit and the shield's gone. Every shot counts now.

*"Concentrate!"* Damian's voice booms. He's not in the simulation—he doesn't need to be. His sharp words always ring in my ears like he lives in my head. *"A shield is useless if you don't activate it on time."*

Shut up, Damian.

I fire into the void. One blast, then another. A shape darts ahead—a Sliman, massive and predatory yet uncannily human looking. Possibly the deadliest hand-eye coordination in the galaxy. Those emerald eyes can track a dust mote at fifty yards, paired with reflexes fast enough to shame a striking cobra—an apex predator engineered with DNA from three different planets to be the ultimate killing machine. My shots clip his shoulder.

He snarls, lunging with a lethal magnetic knife, his eyes burning with fury. His chameleonic skin ripples from green to a mottled brown as he charges at me, a wall of muscle and genetically modified rage. Even in simulation, the raw power rolling off him makes my throat tighten. His movements blur with impossible speed.

"Freya!" Theo's voice again, sharper this time. "Pull left—now!"

I duck and twist, the knife grazing past my ribs. My hand shoots out on instinct, firing a wild blast at the Sliman's exposed flank. He staggers, but before I can finish him off, another emerges.

I sprint for the nearest row of army green tents, weaving through the chaos. A magnetic knife whizzes past my ear, close enough to feel the pull on my hair. I duck again, spin and fire three blind shots. One connects, hitting the Sliman in the leg.

Too late. He's on me, his blow a crushing force that sends my virtual world spiraling into darkness.

*Dead again.*

Damian won't be happy. "*Never performs to her full potential.*" His words sting even in the simulated world. I can picture his disappointed frown, the way his jaw tightens when I fail to meet his impossible standards.

It wasn't by accident that we started calling him *Red*. The nickname fits like a glove.

The pod hisses as it opens. I rip the visor off and un-buckle the straps. The stale, recycled air prickles my nos-trils. Sometimes I can't believe our luck, stumbling onto these abandoned alien facilities then watching Theo and Zoe work their tech magic to get them to function again. Other times, like now, I feel a creeping sense of dread. Are we playing with fire? Tempting fate? Either we'll live long enough to regret it, or we won't live long enough at all.

"That went well," Theo deadpans, scrolling through the data on his touchpad.

And there's... Damian, arms crossed, filling the door-way with his broad shoulders and stormy blue eyes, messy dirty blond hair falling across his forehead.

He steps into my path as soon as he sees me. "Do you know how many shots you missed? You're lucky this is a simulation."

Gods, he really *is* here. This is not a bad dream.

"Yeah, well, lucky me," I mutter, rubbing my temples where the neural feedback throbs like a second heartbeat.

"Your shield failed at forty-eight percent integrity," Theo says, tapping the screen. "You didn't calibrate your angle—again."

*Traitor.* "It's hard to aim when something's trying to rip your throat out, Theo."

Damian exhales hard. "Out there, excuses get everyone killed, not just you."

I force my expression to stay neutral. I'm used to this. Damian's disapproval is mostly background noise now, like the hum of the facility's ventilation system.

"You're done for today," he says, heading for the door.

"Good talk," I mutter under my breath.

Theo finally looks up, his hazel eyes too knowing. "Come back later. I'll fix the calibration and set up another run. Something easier. Maybe target practice."

Bossy sixteen-year-old genius boy with his stupid messy black hair that's practically begging to be ruffled. I resist the urge. "I'll try, Theo."

He frowns. "Do better than try, Freya. None of us are ready. Not even close."

I grab my touchpad and shove past Damian at the door

without looking back.

Theo's right, of course. We aren't ready for real combat. And I'm trailing dead last in a group of twelve.

*"Lacks confidence. Confidence improves focus."*

Damian, ugh. Get out of my head. His voice echoes in my skull like a splinter I can't dig out even as I put growing distance between us.

Finn's words on the other hand are always kind, always reassuring. *"You're as special as any of us, Freya, or you wouldn't be here. It takes courage to even imagine a life beyond the plantations."*

Sweet, steady, stubborn Finn. My best friend. My rock. The problem is I know the truth. I know I clung to the idea of freedom back at the plantation not because I was brave, but because I was desperate, terrified of spending another day under alien control. *"Knowing one's weaknesses is the ultimate strength,"* Finn always says. But sometimes knowing you are the weakest link just confirms what you've always feared: you're the one who might get everyone killed.

Outside, the camp sprawls beneath the canopy of redwoods, a mix of alien tech and makeshift survivalism. Rabbit darts between dummies in the combat ring, practicing evasive maneuvers. The sharp clang of metal echoes from the tech lair. Zoe, Theo's partner in crime, is probably knee-deep in another experiment that might blow us all sky high.

I need air. Space. Anywhere away from drills and tension and Damian's constant glare.

Before I can disappear into the trees, Rabbit intercepts me. His usual energy bounces off him like sparks.

Right. I promised to teach him different types of knots today. One of my few useful skills—water knots, square knots, Palomar knots. Give me a piece of rope, and I'll bend it to my will.

The old alien facilities consist of eight separate buildings arranged in a perfect semicircle around an open space that we use for training. We call it the combat ring. The invaders cleared a chunk of the forest to make room for their austere architecture.

We've made these facilities our home for two years now. Best we can figure, the aliens abandoned them long ago because the dense forest canopy scrambled some of their precious frequencies, making communication with the plantations shaky at times.

They relocated their operations a hundred miles south, where they built their new headquarters, leaving us an unintentional gift—forgotten technology that our tech people, Theo and Zoe, coaxed back to life with their endless patience and clever minds. Even better, the same forest that disrupted alien signals now shields us from their radar sweeps and tracking systems. Nature, it turns out, makes a pretty good ally when you're trying to stay invisible.

"What's your battle score this time?" Rabbit asks, bouncing on the balls of his feet. His rope is looped around his neck like a scarf.

I force a smile. "Never mind that. It's peaceful out here, isn't it?"

He doesn't push, holding up his rope instead. "Knots today, right? You promised."

I sigh, glancing toward the forest. "Yeah, sure. And try to dial down the bouncing. It's making my head spin." Truth is his endless energy helps drown out the nagging little voices in my head.

We leave the facilities and head back to the surrounding forest. The path to our tents winds through towering redwoods with branches that interlace overhead, filtering the sunlight. Six hundred steps to the place we call home.

Rabbit chatters beside me about silly dreams and impossible plans. He's good at that—making you forget reality for a moment. He can spend twenty minutes gushing about the way morning dew catches light as if the alien invasion never happened.

"Just wait until we take Plantation-6," he says, his voice bubbling with excitement. "Kicky and Mendy, their eyes are gonna pop right out of their heads when they see me!"

Plantation-6. The place where he'd been harvested, trained and punished for breathing wrong. We all carry our own custom-made plantation horror stories with our names on them.

Except they weren't names. His friends, Kicky and Mendy, were really 6-57849A76 and 6-57940A57. We've all been tempted, at one point or another, to give names to the friends we left behind and imagine the day we'll march back and set them free.

Our alien masters didn't permit names. We were numbers branded on the backs of our necks in precise black script. Those numbers identified us to the guards and determined our work detail. That's why they kept our hair cropped to two inches—nothing could hide those numbers. Nothing could hide what we were.

As we reach the east edge of the camp we go straight to my tent, which is nestled between Finn's and Rabbit's. I need to get more rope and strings for our lesson. Our three tents are the only ones occupied here. The other Saviors keep to the west side, near the water well and the crops and the escape tunnel, hidden beneath layers of vines.

Rabbit looks smaller than usual in his dirt-smudged shirt and pants.

"Have you been running in the hills again?" I ask.

He shrugs, which is answer enough. He can't resist scaling the southern bluffs despite Damian's endless warnings. Up there, where our compound shrinks to a toy village, he finds something we lost long ago—freedom. Or at least the illusion of it.

Rabbit's the youngest Savior at thirteen, undersized for his age, all whipcord muscle and restless energy. What he lacks in size, he makes up for in pure speed. He dreams of the far-off lands where cheetahs once roamed free, of wide-open spaces where nothing could catch him.

He can outrun everything—the wind, the Sliman patrols, the nightmares of Plantation-6. He is our own cheetah, our fleeting hope in a world that feels increasingly dark.

Outside my tent, I show him how to tie a water knot, but his fingers move ahead of my instructions, tying and untying with fluid grace. He's grown so much since Finn and I took him under our wing, drawn to his infectious optimism.

There are fifteen plantations in our district. Beyond that? We might as well be blind. More plantations? Other rebels? The toxic craters surrounding the district make sure we'll never know. If it weren't for the library ruins in Lost Town—a treasure trove of knowledge the first Saviors stumbled upon years ago—we wouldn't even know for sure there was a *before*.

Everything in our district has been destroyed, pulverized, brought down by the alien invaders and their mutant armies, the terrifying Sliman. To survive, we must stay out of their way. We ghost past areas with surveillance cameras, dodge radars and are extremely careful to never run into Sliman patrols. They might not know about our plans or what we call ourselves, but they know we are gone, and they are always on the hunt.

"What do you think it's like?" Rabbit asks suddenly.

I pause mid-knot, glancing at him. "What's what like?"

"Freedom." He stares toward the forest, where the trees stretch endlessly. "Real freedom. Not just running, hiding. Actually *living*."

His words twist something in my chest. "I don't know," I say finally. "But I guess it starts with not giving up."

Rabbit goes still. His attention shifts to something behind me.

"It might take everything we have to win back the world," Damian's voice cuts through the quiet, "including a few lengths of rope."

I turn to see Damian striding toward us with Daphne at his heels.

Huh... These two are thick as thieves and rarely venture to our side of the camp, the *wrong* side, too far from the facilities and their precious escape tunnel... too close to the wild heart of the forest.

What they don't seem to get is that this corner is ours because it works for us. The trees keep us cool when summer bakes the compound. When the deer that graze nearby run, we are alerted to possible danger. We've carved out our own slice of almost-normal, even if it's just pretend.

Daphne's eyes catch on the rope in my hands, then drift to my half-carved boat on the ground, its hull curved like a crescent moon. I can read the judgment in her eyes, the unspoken accusation that I'm wasting time, wasting potential, and dragging Rabbit down with me.

"So, this is how the alien empire falls?" Daphne says, her lips curled into an arrogant smirk that only she could pull off.

I roll my eyes and finish the noose I've been working on since I saw them approaching. I'd love to test it on those perfect legs of hers and drag *her* down for once, but I'd need Damian's strength for that. And probably his permission too.

Daphne's smirk fades. We've never been best friends, far from it, but I can't deny what she is: the strongest girl I've ever seen, deadly with any weapon she touches. She dominates most of us in training, taking us down with brutal efficiency. And then there's her real gift—psychic abilities that can save us from fatal mistakes in battle or strip our thoughts bare like peeling paint. It frustrates her to no end that her powers slide right off me like rain, leaving her blind to whatever's in my head.

"If you're so interested in what we do, Daphne, why don't you move over here? We could always make room." I toss her my freshly tied noose with a sweet smile.

She holds the noose up, her eyes widening a little before she tosses it aside. "You're such a child."

Damian shakes his head. "Meeting in twenty minutes, in the Armory."

At twenty-one, our fearless leader is the oldest in the group—probably the oldest free person alive. Tall with strength to match the Sliman mutants themselves, he's brilliant at strategic planning, but diplomacy? That's a language Damian never learned.

Rabbit blasts away in a blur before I can even get to my feet. We all watch as leaves settle in his wake, dancing back to earth.

"I'll be there," I say, gathering up the practice knots.

"Don't be late," Daphne sneers. "Though with your track record, you'll probably miss the one meeting that actually matters to you." She stalks after Rabbit, her long strides eating up the distance between them.

That... was more bizarre than usual.

Damian steps closer. "Nothing's been decided. We wanted you involved in the process," he says, a rare tenderness in his tone.

"Damian, what is it?"

My question confuses him. "I thought—we assumed Rabbit told you."

"Told me what?" A sinking feeling settles in my stomach.

"Finn is missing."

# Chapter 2

"FINN'S TOUCHPAD SIGNAL HAS gone static," Damian says. His voice echoes off the Armory walls lined with our precious few weapons and ammunition crates. "No movement. He should've been back hours ago."

The words don't make sense at first. Finn? Static? Finn is *never* late. Never still. *Keep moving* is practically his motto.

My fingers press against my temples. "What do you mean he's not moving?"

Theo shoves his touchpad into my hands. A single red dot pulses at the edge of our district, dangerously close to the toxic mud crater that separates us from the wastelands and whatever lies beyond them. Way too close.

"His last check-in was here," Theo says. "Then nothing. He's just sitting there."

"That's impossible," I mutter. "He knows better than

to go anywhere near the crater. He *wrote* the damn protocols on crater safety."

"There are no crater protocols," Rabbit pipes up from a corner.

I glare daggers at him. He just shrugs.

Twenty-four hours. Finn's been gone twenty-four hours on a routine perimeter scan, volunteering like he always does.

*"Just a quick two-mile sweep,"* he said before he left, that crooked smile of his making it sound like a casual stroll in the park. *"Mapping out changes, looking for unusual activity."*

Standard stuff. Safe stuff. Or it should have been.

I glance at Damian and Daphne, the two most seasoned members of the Saviors. They stand apart, both stronger, more skilled and more lethal than any of us. They should have been the ones out there with their enhanced reflexes and battle-tested instincts. But that's not how Finn operates. His sense of duty is a force of nature—constant, unrelenting, impossible to argue with. Where Damian leads with a level head and plans with cold precision, Finn leads with his heart, shields us with his entire being. It's what drives him. What makes him *Finn*.

I shouldn't be upset that he's willing to take risks. We're all walking targets anyway, every second of every day. Yet, anger sparks within me. At Finn for his constant need to put himself in danger. At myself for always letting him.

For *needing* him.

My reaction is a little hypocritical, because Finn has protected me all my life. He's the reason I'm even part of the Saviors. Without him, I'd still be just another number.

Where he is, I should be. That's the one truth I've never doubted. And now he's out there, alone, and I'm stuck here, useless.

Damian crosses his arms. "If he doesn't show by nightfall, we'll go looking for him. The Sliman have been edging too close lately."

"Nightfall? No, no way." The words leave my mouth before I can stop them. "We have to find him now."

Damian's eyes narrow. "In broad daylight? And risk exposing ourselves? We could be walking right into a trap. You know the stakes, Freya."

"We can't just leave him out there, Damian."

"Freya," he snaps, his tone ice-cold. "We wait. That's an order."

"Finn wouldn't wait."

"That's why I'm the leader and he's not." Damian turns to Theo. "Set up another sweep of the perimeter. If there's movement, I want to know about it immediately."

My hands clench into fists. Rabbit shoots me a worried glance, but I'm already moving. If I stay in this room one more second, I might actually throw something at Damian.

The air outside is thick and heavy with late summer

heat. Sweat forms at my temples and slides down the back of my neck.

Finn and I come from the same breeding village and the same plantation. We were transferred separately to Plantation-8 when we turned seven years old, Finn a year ahead of me, leaving our mothers and younger siblings behind in the breeding village, where children were born and sorted like products on an assembly line. Ever since, Finn has been there for me, has given me part of his food ration when I felt weak, has tucked me in and stroked my hair when I couldn't sleep.

Finn escaped the plantation when he was fifteen, trusting that the whispers about a rebel band of teens were true. He ran, and for over a year, I didn't know whether he was alive or dead.

Life without Finn was a hollow grind. I performed my duties—cleaning, cooking, and endless combat training under the Sliman guards' watchful eyes. We were fed pills and booster shots, drilled on how to strengthen our bodies through mental control.

We went through relentless testing—physical endurance, mental sharpness, combat precision. We learned to read and write. Every failure brought swift and brutal discipline. The Sliman guards wielded their sensory receptor devices like instruments of torment. Electricity and invasive lasers delivered pain sharp enough to drop us to our knees but never left a mark.

On the outside, I was a perfect cog in their system. But every night, my fury boiled over. I would punch my pillow, bite it, scream into it, releasing everything I couldn't show during the day. Trapped in that hellhole without Finn, survival felt like a slow death.

Still, I was happy for him. He'd escaped. I clung to the hope that he had found something better, something worth the trouble. But when he came back for me, risking everything, I realized that he wasn't just looking for something better. He wanted to share it with *me*.

The night Finn returned, I was nearly fifteen, my childhood stripped away by years of training and control. Hope was a distant, fragile thing I no longer dared to reach for.

I had just stepped into my dorm room, the one I shared with four other girls. It was late in the evening, and the others were still in the common area, squeezing out the last scraps of our allotted social time. I wasn't one for socializing, and Finn had bet on that.

He grabbed me from behind before I could see him, his hand clamping over my mouth.

"It's Finn," he whispered urgently, his breath hot against my ear. "Don't scream."

The name meant nothing to me. He loosened his grip, spinning me around to face him. I almost let out a cry despite his warning.

"Ace!" I whispered. "Why do you call yourself Finn?"

We used to call each other names when no one else was listening. Ace for his quick reflexes, Tick for my ticklishness. It wasn't fair—his nickname was cool, mine wasn't—but it was our secret.

He scanned me from head to toe, his green eyes sharp, assessing as if trying to determine whether it was truly little Tick he had in front of him.

"No time to explain," he said at last. "We have to get out of here."

"Out of here? You mean the plantation? That's impossible. They have rotating scanning cameras now. Everything's changed since you escaped." My voice broke. "*Because* you escaped."

"Everything is possible, Tick. Just tell me one thing. Do you trust me?"

I looked at him, really looked. He wasn't the boy I remembered. He was taller now, harder, his frame lean but strong, his skin bronzed from sun and wind. His eyes burned with a confidence I barely recognized. But he'd come back for me. That much hadn't changed.

I swallowed hard. "Of course I trust you."

His hand reached for mine, and I took it without hesitation. I felt something stir in my chest. Not quite hope, but something close.

We slipped out through the back window. Crawling low to the ground, we inched forward. The damp earth clung to my hands and knees. Every sound—a snapping twig, the rustle of leaves—felt magnified in the silence. What we were attempting seemed absurd, impossible. Any second, I expected the Sliman to pounce on us.

Finn paused, pulling a small touchpad from his pocket. He keyed in a sequence of numbers as the faint blue glow of the screen illuminated his face. Overhead, the rotating cameras stopped abruptly, and their mechanical hum faded into silence.

"How did you do that?" My voice was barely audible over the pounding of my heart.

Finn glanced at me with a smug grin on his muddied face. "A little magic."

Magic or not, it worked. The Sliman patrols, relying on their new state-of-the-art scanning cameras, were fewer now. The cameras monitored every inch of the plantation within seconds, detecting movement, sound, even the slightest variations in light. Anything unusual would trigger an immediate alert to the Director's office.

"With change comes opportunity," Finn would later say of that night. When the plantations beefed up their scanning precision technology, they relaxed on their physical security measures and Finn had found a way to exploit that.

We crouched for a moment longer before Finn motioned for me to follow. Rising to our feet, we broke into a sprint, heading straight for the electric, twenty-foot fence. My legs burned as I pushed forward.

Ahead of us was an opening in the fence, oddly precise, just wide enough for us to squeeze through. On the other side, holding the cut wires, stood the most severe and beautiful girl I had ever seen. Her long blonde hair shimmered in the night wind like spun gold, and her eyes glowed with an eerie intensity, bright even in the shadows. The first time you see Daphne, you never forget it. She looked like she belonged to the darkness itself, a nocturnal creature out hunting.

"Quick," she said. "The electricity will come back any moment now."

Finn darted through first and I hesitated, momentarily mesmerized by Daphne's otherworldly presence, before forcing myself to follow. I stumbled through the gap, nearly colliding with a tall, broad-shouldered guy standing on the other side.

Damian.

He didn't so much as glance at me, his focus razor-sharp as he worked. Together, he and Daphne reconnected the severed wires. A thin blue laser flickered from Damian's touchpad as he fused the cut ends seamlessly back into place. Within seconds, the electric field roared back to life.

The distant plantation lights began to spin as I became lightheaded. My legs buckled, but before I hit the ground, Damian hoisted me effortlessly over his shoulder and began to run.

His grip was steady, unyielding, as if carrying my weight

was no more difficult than hauling a sack of supplies.

The dark forest closed in around us. I felt like I was floating down a river of trees and moonlight. The sweat on his neck smelled sharp like exotic fruit, tangerines, maybe. My thoughts blurred with each step until I faded into sleep, lulled by the rhythm of his movement and the growing distance from the plantation.

The next thing I remember is being surrounded by the Saviors and the soft glow of a campfire. They told me I had slept for hours. That's when I realized Damian's extraordinary strength. He had carried me through rough terrain half the night.

Only later would I guess the whole truth: Daphne had hypnotized me. At the time, I thought it was Damian's quiet resolve and his steady arms that had made the chaos of the escape feel almost safe.

The others gathered to meet me with curious faces. Finn stayed by my side, but the swarm of introductions and questions overwhelmed me. I fell asleep again as the sun came up and slept all day.

When I woke, the silver glow of the moon pierced through the treetops. For the first time in my life, there were no guards, no drills, no harsh lights or blaring alarms. It was my first *freedom sleep*—pure, uninterrupted, and more peaceful than any dream I had dared to imagine.

I sat up in the small tent. Outside, a shadow stretched across the ground. Finn. He was silhouetted against the moonlight, his figure familiar and reassuring.

We talked for hours, my questions spilling out faster than he could answer them. I wanted to know everything—how he escaped, how he survived, why he came back. Most of all, I wanted to know why he called himself Finn now, not Ace.

When I finally asked, his face grew serious. "I'll show you tomorrow," he said and left it at that.

At dawn, Finn led me through the woods to the crumbling remains of Lost Town. Half-destroyed buildings jutted like broken teeth from the earth, their walls cracked and stained with time. Vines crawled over rusted signs. Shattered glass and debris littered the ground.

"Human and alien forces fought here," Finn explained as we walked. "It wasn't just a battle—it was a massacre. Every human who resisted was killed or enslaved. Children were taken to the plantations."

He stopped in front of a building with half its roof caved in, its entrance twisted and sagging. Lost Town hadn't been rebuilt or erased. It had been left to rot, swallowed by the surrounding woods.

Finn's face darkened as he looked at the ruins. "This is where it started," he said softly. "My new life. What I became."

Finn guided me inside the building. My eyes adjusted quickly to the dim light filtering through broken windows. Books lay scattered everywhere, some crumpled and torn, others precariously stacked on damaged shelves.

"Watch your step," Finn said. He gestured to the books piled on the floor. "This was a place of knowledge. A library."

I followed him deeper inside, careful where I placed my feet. A few books were laid out on tables. Finn glanced at them, his tone sharpening. "Don't touch those."

As we walked through the aisles, I noticed that some books on the shelves stood out. They were cleaner, their covers free of the thick dust that cloaked the others.

"This is it," Finn said, stopping in front of a crooked shelf. "You can choose any book here. Pick the name you like best from inside. If nothing speaks to you, move to the next one. Keep going until you find it."

I stared at the rows of books with their cracked and faded spines, some barely holding together.

"We're reborn when we leave the plantations," Finn said, "and every birth requires a new name."

He reached for a book and handed it to me. Its cover was worn but intact, the title stamped in bold letters: *The Adventures of Huckleberry Finn.*

"This is my book," he said. "Where I found my name."

I turned the book over in my hands. "Why didn't you take it with you?"

His green eyes shadowed. "Everything must remain as it is here. There can be no sign of change. We can never be too careful."

I didn't have the heart to tell him that even I had spotted the cleaner books and the faint fingerprints left behind by the Saviors. Finn might want to believe the secret was invisible, but even Tick, his little ticklish shadow, could spot where their hands had lingered.

In theory, he was right. Sliman scouts can pick up the smallest details and inconsistencies. The Saviors had been lucky so far. Lost Town was a dead place to the Sliman, overlooked and abandoned. But luck was fragile, and every trip back carried risk.

I scanned the shelves for several minutes. My fingers hesitated over titles until one caught my eye. *World Mythology.*

Finn wasn't happy with the size of that book. He raised an eyebrow. "That's seven hundred pages. Are you sure? That's the one you want to start with?"

I nodded, drawn to the book in a way I couldn't explain. Finn sighed but didn't argue. He knew that look in my eyes.

He took me back to the library every day and watched as I devoured the book's contents. Every story filled the blank spaces in my mind with wonder. Gods, heroes and monsters swept me into worlds long gone, worlds I hadn't known existed.

And then I found it.

"Freya," I said as my fingers traced the name on the page. "Queen of the Valkyries. Warrior goddess."

Finn studied me. "Really?"

"Really," I said firmly. This name, *Freya,* felt like something I could grow into. A promise to myself. I felt connected to something bigger than my own past. Something powerful and thrilling.

The memories crash over me now as I pace outside the Armory, trying to drown out the questions that won't stop screaming in my head. Where is Finn? Is he hurt? Trapped? Worse? The not-knowing feels like an impossible weight on my chest.

The forest whispers to me, dark and alive with secrets. Damian would want me to stay put.

But the thing about being named after a warrior goddess? Sometimes you have to make your own rules.

I slip into the trees like a shadow.

# Chapter 3

THE ANCIENT REDWOODS SWALLOW me whole as I trace familiar winding paths. For once, I'm not counting my steps or scanning for drone activity. I'm not looking for edible berries or cataloguing escape routes. I'm just walking, breathing and trying to push down the panic clawing at my throat.

Finn... The thought of him drags me back to the breeding village, to my mother, my brother, my two sisters. Their faces are blurry now, faded like old photographs, but I carry them with me, shadows that never leave.

We didn't know our fathers. The men were kept in separate housing on the far side of the village, most of them nameless faces who labored in the fields. The divide was absolute—no visits, no shared meals, no recognition.

I was four when they came for my brother. *Harvested* was the term they used, as if children were nothing more than crops to be collected. I still remember his hand squeezing mine before they pulled him away.

All children are harvested when they turn seven. My sisters must have been taken by now too. And my mother... she must be alone, if she's even alive. Her health was already failing when they took me eleven years ago, and the alien invaders only keep the fittest for the breeding labs. If she's no longer useful, she's likely been cast aside.

The day they harvested my brother, my mother's face was blank, devoid of emotion. She planted a kiss on his forehead, told him to be a good boy and then went back to her tasks as if nothing had happened. She mentioned my brother, her son, once or twice the next morning and then seemed to have moved on.

Her reaction was not surprising. That was what survival looked like in the breeding village. The adults were hollow shells, stripped of anything resembling will and agency. They didn't question, didn't resist. Their speech was clipped to the bare minimum. They lived to complete their daily tasks. The women raised their children until they were harvested, and then... nothing. No rebellion, no grief. Just quiet obedience.

Once, I found a book about zombies in the library. The descriptions haunted me, reminded me of the mothers in the village. Not dead, but not truly alive either. Walking ghosts who'd had everything that made them human scraped away.

We talk about this sometimes at the camp, trading theories about what the aliens did to them. Doc, who earned his nickname for working and training in the medical labs at Plantation-4, has seen firsthand what horrors they're capable of. At seventeen, he's already witnessed more than most of us could stomach: genetic manipulation, DNA splicing, mind control. According to him, they're not just creating new species like the Sliman mutants; they're perfecting the ability to control minds, suppressing thought and desire until nothing remains.

Finn has a different theory. He found an old medical book in the library that mentioned something called *lobotomy*—the closest human equivalent to what the aliens have done, surgically removing the parts of the brain that make us human.

Rabbit hates this theory with a burning passion. He needs to believe his mother can be saved, that whatever was done to her can be undone. "No one's taking pieces of her brain," he insists. "She's *still* in there. She has to be."

I want to believe him. I want him to be right. But belief feels fragile and slippery like ice right now.

The forest around me is dense and quiet. A metallic flash in the undergrowth catches my eye and I freeze mid-step. My muscles tense as training kicks in. *Notice anything that doesn't belong.* And this? This definitely doesn't belong.

Slowly, I crouch and reach for it—a thin sheet of flexible metal, half-buried in leaves. My hands shake as I pull it free.

It looks like some kind of digital map. The material feels smooth, almost alive under my fingers. Alien tech. The topography glows with faint blue lines, showing terrain I've never seen mapped before. Areas beyond the toxic craters, regions we believed were dangerous wastelands, impossible to chart.

I clutch the map to my chest, my thoughts racing. Sliman scouts don't just lose tech. If they're close enough to drop something this vital in our woods, Finn's disappearance could be more than just bad luck.

I break into a run, weaving through the trees toward the Armory. Maybe I hate Damian's inflexibility, maybe I want to scream at his stubborn face, but he needs to see this.

I burst through the Armory's heavy metal door with the map tucked under my shirt. The musty air hits my nostrils, thick with tension. Everyone's crammed together around something I can't see.

My heart still pounds from the sprint, but I push my way through the crowd and then I stop cold in my tracks.

I must be hallucinating.

Finn sits on a chair smack in the middle of it all, very much alive but looking like something the wasteland chewed up and spit out for good measure.

His face is covered in bruises, cuts and dried blood. His black shirt—or what's left of it—hangs in tatters, and his usually neat chestnut hair is a wild tangled mess.

Doc kneels beside him, cutting strips of precious bandages to wrap Finn's mangled hands.

"Nobody touch him!" Doc barks as his eyes snap up to mine. "He just got back. I haven't had a chance to assess the extent of his injuries yet."

I stop where I am, rooted to the spot, afraid to throw my arms around him, afraid my affection will hurt him more. "Finn, you stupid boy, what did you get yourself into?" I whisper.

He has the audacity to chuckle, then winces halfway through. "Just that, Tick. Something stupid." His voice is so low I can barely hear him. "I was trying to get to a rare flower, slipped on some rocks and fell down a deep ravine. Lost my touchpad to a huge bird on the way down. Had a hell of a time crawling back up."

*A bird.* That explains how his touchpad ended up near the crater then.

The words come out flat, disbelieving. "A rare flower?"

Finn pulls away from Doc's careful ministrations and shoves his battered hand into his pocket. He slowly pulls out a crumpled purple flower. The color is glorious, deep and rich, even in its reduced state.

Tilly, one of the younger Saviors, edges closer to examine the flower. Her eyes widen with wonder.

"It's beautiful," she says. "Have you ever seen such color?"

"I got it for you, Freya," Finn says, locking his eyes on mine.

"Oh," I say. "A rare flower from a rare idiot."

Finn grins, and even as Doc swats his shoulder in frustration, I see that spark, that unshakable Finn-ness that no amount of pain can subdue.

Rabbit and Biscuit hurry to join Tilly, clustering around Finn like excited puppies. It's hard to stay mad at him with his fan club in full force, but I'm determined to try.

Tilly takes the flower from Finn and presses it into my hands. It's beautiful and broken just like Finn. He'll get himself killed trying to protect everyone, trying to be thoughtful every second of the day, trying to bring beauty into a brutal world that knows only how to destroy it.

"What do you think?" he says softly.

I glare into his bright, impossibly green eyes and resist the urge to slap him. "You know what I think."

My glare is sharp enough to make Rabbit and Biscuit shuffle back, but Finn just watches me, his grin unwavering, as if my frustration amuses him. As if getting himself half-killed is all some kind of game.

I tear my gaze away and turn to Damian who's leaning against the weapons rack, arms crossed over his chest.

I take a breath and walk up to him. My hand slips under

my shirt, gripping the map. When I reach Damian, I pull it free, holding it out between us.

Damian arches an eyebrow. "What am I looking at?"

"Alien tech. A map."

His brows knit together as he takes it from me. The faint blue lines glow brighter under the Armory lights. "Where did you find this?"

I hesitate, glancing around at the curious faces pressing closer. "In the forest."

"Just now? You went out there *alone* after I explicitly—"

"Of course she did," Daphne cuts in. "She *lives* to defy you, Damian, you know that. Oh, and to play the hero."

"I wasn't—" I start, but Damian cuts me off.

"You disobeyed direct orders." His eyes lock on mine as red creeps up his cheeks. "You could've been spotted, or worse. If Sliman scouts were that close—"

"It doesn't matter," I snap, louder than I mean to. "The map, Damian, that's what matters. It's real, and we have it because I went out there. Or would you rather the Sliman retrieved it?"

The room falls silent as my words settle over the group. Damian hands the map to the tech experts, Theo and Zoe.

"This doesn't match any map we've seen," Zoe says. "If these readings are accurate, then everything we know might be a lie."

"It is," I reply. "It's beyond the craters—districts we

thought were uninhabitable, nothing more than dead zones. Look at all the green, the water sources..."

The murmurs grow louder around us as the other Saviors lean in, curiosity overriding their patience. Biscuit steps closer, practically scaling Damian's back to get a closer look.

Daphne's frown deepens, but she doesn't say anything.

"If this is legitimate," Damian says, his voice low and measured, "we need a plan, and fast. Everyone, get some rest. And Freya? Don't test me again."

I bite back a retort, clenching the flower in my hand as Damian walks away to speak with Doc.

"So..." Finn's weak cough draws attention back to his chair. "My *foolish* adventure had perfect timing after all?"

"Don't push it, Finn," I warn him, but there's no anger left in my voice. Because he's right—the map could change everything. And judging by the shadow that crosses his face now, he knows it too.

# Chapter 4

It's getting dark and the heat hasn't broken yet. The only relief comes from the redwoods behind my tent, where their shadows stretch like cool fingers across the ground. I sit by the gnarled roots of one of the older giant trees, taking in the evening scents and sounds, replaying the day's events in my mind—Finn's brush with death and that damn map, as if I can rewind the tape and stop the Sliman from ever getting close. It's the *closest* they've ever been to our camp and the thought is unsettling.

Doc startles me as he emerges from the shadows like a ghost. "Finn's fine," he says with a smile. He looks around aimlessly, as if he's forgotten what he was looking for, before he repeats, "He will be just fine."

I nod and start picking at my fingernails, a nervous habit I can't shake. "I heard you the first time," I say just to tease him.

"You're right, I'm sorry," he says as he lowers himself onto the ground next to me. His brown eyes are as warm as ever. That's Doc—apologizing even when he hasn't done anything wrong. He's probably the kindest soul left in this broken world.

I nudge him with my elbow. "Doc, I'm just messing with you."

"Well, you'll be thrilled to know that we're having a training session in a few minutes," he says, his gaze shifting to my fingernails. "And you should probably stop biting those nails. It's not exactly hygienic."

"Back up. Training? In this heat, this late?"

"Don't shoot the messenger," Doc says, raising his arms in mock surrender. "It wasn't my idea."

"Let me guess. Daphne?"

Doc gets to his feet, brushing dirt from his pants. "Just come to the combat ring, Freya. It'll be... educational."

Training with everyone watching is never fun for me. I always feel like the only one without any special skills. I pull out my knife and grab a piece of wood, carving to keep my hands busy. At least I'm good at this—making useless things.

Barely ten minutes pass before more footsteps crunch through leaves and twigs. I know it can't be Finn; no one can ever hear Finn coming. He moves like a cat and he's more flexible than a rubber band. Still, I catch myself hoping it's him.

Instead, Damian shows up. "Why are you still here?" His eyes catch on the small wooden boat taking shape in my hands.

Yep, delaying the inevitable was a bad idea. I should have just gone to training and gotten through it.

"I was about to come and find you," I say, tucking the knife into my pocket as I get to my feet.

I walk past him, hoping he's not in lecture mode.

"What about your boat?" he says.

"What?" I turn, surprised. My little half-finished boat is in his hand. "I don't want it," I say. "I make one every day. I don't keep them."

Damian shrugs. "Maybe I'll keep this one."

"Suit yourself," I say, baffled by his interest in a badly made toy.

At the combat ring, the Saviors are sitting down in a circle. Damian plops down next to Daphne. I take a quick glance at Finn before I sit next to Zoe. His head and hands are bandaged but he seems to be doing okay, all things considered.

"So, what's going on?" I say, hoping they haven't all been waiting for me.

"Not much," Zoe says. "I'm updating stats before we train."

With that, the Saviors begin to rise, each making their way to their favorite spot in the ring. I linger with Zoe, watching her work.

"Can I see?" I say.

"Sure." She hands me her touchpad. The screen displays a series of records and charts.

I scroll through monthly numbers before switching to individual skills and progress charts.

Rabbit's name pops up first. Nothing new here. The kid is a walking ball of energy.

Next in line is Scout. She's fifteen and she didn't quite pick her name herself. It was more of a collective decision after the group located the book *To Kill a Mockingbird* at the library and, well, the name fit perfectly. Scout can track like a bloodhound. If there's any mark or scent or print, she'll find it. She has uncanny orientation skills and can read the stars in the sky like a road map.

Biscuit's stats show up next. He's fifteen like Scout and he can pick up smells from miles away. Doc says his olfactory nerve is a miracle of evolution, that hounds would kill to have it. The problem is, Biscuit's supernatural sense of smell has one major flaw: the first thing he senses always, *always*, is food. If there's anything edible within a mile radius, he'll find it. And he'll eat it. Which is not particularly good news for the rest of us.

Doc's profile follows, and it's sparse compared to his actual value to us. Sure, it lists his medical training from Plantation-4, but it doesn't capture how many times his steady hands have pieced us back together, how many bones he's set, how many wounds he's stitched closed while telling terrible jokes to distract us. He might be the most important Savior, though he'd never admit it.

Nya's stats are impressive as always—an accomplished archer, perfect accuracy scores, unprecedented simulation results, and she *loves* blowing things up. Her shock bow might as well be an extension of her arm; she even sleeps with it within reach. At sixteen, she's all angles and wire-strong muscle, with coal-dark eyes that burn when she's angry. Which is often. The only thing bigger than her talent for destroying things is her stubborn streak.

Tilly's file makes me smile. Fourteen years old, with vision and hearing cranked up to impossible levels—some kind of neural implants from infancy, Doc thinks. But the stats don't mention how she fills silence with stories, how her constant chatter makes our dark world feel a little lighter. Sometimes I seek her out just to listen to her talk.

Zoe and Theo are the reason we're here at all, the reason why we were able to claim this patch of forest and turn the alien technology of the abandoned facilities into survival tools: solar panels, computers, touchpad radars, simulators, satellite control systems, electromagnetic accelerators, high-energy liquid lasers—in their hands, science becomes something like magic.

Theo's only sixteen, but he's a tech genius, trained to operate and create digital systems, a true prodigy if ever there was one. Give him any piece of technology, and he'll have it dancing to his code within hours.

Zoe's profile is enough to make my head spin. At nineteen, she's got the kind of brain that makes quantum physics look like simple addition. We joke about watching for steam coming from her ears when she's deep in calculations. She and Theo escaped Plantation-1 together. Maybe that's why they move like two parts of the same machine, anticipating each other's thoughts before they're spoken.

Zoe and Daphne are close friends. They're both nineteen, both brilliant in their own ways. Maybe that's what started their connection. Maybe Zoe is drawn to Daphne's strength and resolve. Or maybe I'll never know why, and maybe there are things about friendship I'll never understand.

My finger hovers over Daphne's profile, but I'm not ready to read about her perfect combat scores, her flawless mission records. Not today.

We all know how to fight, some better than others, we're resourceful and we've learned to survive in the harshest conditions. But it's not just about individual skills. We're nothing without each other. Alone, we'd just be stray animals living day to day, lost and without direction, if it wasn't for the Saviors.

Our training began in the plantations, intense, relentless, for reasons we still don't understand. The alien directors pushed us to our limits, demanded we become stronger, faster, smarter. Then, like clockwork, kids would vanish between seventeen and nineteen.

Some we know ended up back in the breeding villages, minds hollowed out, pasts erased, walking through their days like ghosts. The rest? That's the question that keeps us up at night.

I drag myself to the combat ring. Finn's already there, tossing a pulse gun my way. I snatch it from the air as muscle memory takes over.

"Can't do much today," he says. "Doc's watching me like a hawk. He insists I take it easy." A flicker of a smile crosses his face. "Do you want to practice target shooting?"

I shrug. Why not? I'm not sure I'm completely over my frustration at him for risking his life all the time, but Finn, unlike Daphne, never turns these things into a competition. He will allow me to train at my own pace without judgement or pressure.

My shots find their mark more often than not, close to eighty percent accuracy. Finn pats me on the shoulder, but I can't find it in me to return his smile. I've always felt a little like an outcast when it comes to showing off my skills. Because unlike the others, I know what I am.

I'm the only Savior who had to be saved. Ironic, isn't it?

Everyone else fought their way out of the plantations, brave enough to believe in something bigger, strong enough to grab their freedom with both hands. But me? I just got lucky.

The whispers had been there for years—stories passed in hushed voices about bands of fugitives living free in the woods and mountains. No one knows how the rumors started, but they gave us kids hope, something to dream about in the sterile halls of the plantations.

As far as we know, we're the only fugitive band, at least in this plantation district. There might be others out there in the world. I *hope* there are, and the map suggests it's more likely than we thought, but we've never heard of them. We're always on the lookout for more fugitives. Scout was our last rescue, ten months ago, and each day without finding more feels like a wasted day.

But maybe that's just me, the girl who couldn't save herself, trying to make up for it by saving others.

After training, we gather around the bonfire, steam rising from our soup bowls while we discuss security protocols and patrol schedules. Finn's ordeal and the map have changed things—we need new strategies, better defenses.

Theo and Zoe huddle over their touchpads, preparing to present their latest battle simulation. The firelight catches their intent faces as they whisper back and forth, tweaking variables.

Finn takes advantage of the quiet moment to come and sit beside me, close enough that our shoulders almost touch.

"Have you completely forgiven me yet?" he says.

I shake my head slowly, deliberately, making sure he sees

every nanometer of that *no*.

"Okay, then what percentage of forgiveness are we talking about?"

I lift my eyes up to his. "You can't charm your way out of everything, Finn."

"There's something else bothering you, Tick." It's not a question.

"I'm fine, Finn. A bit melancholic, that's all. And these endless meetings aren't helping when all you want is some peace and quiet."

"Meetings are a necessary evil, Freya. Our partnership, our trust in each other—that's all we've got. We need to think as one. In battle, it could mean the difference between life and death."

I grab a stick, scratching numbers in the dirt before they shift into the outline of a face—a woman's face. My mother's? Mine? I start to add a mustache, but Finn's hand catches mine, warm and steady.

"You think Damian's stronger than me, but I have my own set of skills. I'm in no more danger when I go out than he or Daphne would be."

I know all about Finn's skills. I've seen the way he moves like liquid through combat forms, how he scales rocks, walls and redwoods like gravity isn't a thing. His mastery of complex high-energy lasers for long-distance targeting is a feat that leaves even Daphne impressed.

At nineteen, Finn's abilities make most of us look

clumsy in comparison.

But Damian... he's different. Nearly a head taller than Finn, two years older, and six years into freedom. His strength rivals a Sliman's, and in close combat, no one comes close—not even Daphne. Damian is a force of nature.

I don't want to tell Finn that his skills are exactly what worries me. That they make him overconfident, and they make him take risks that even Damian wouldn't attempt. That every time he disappears into the forest, I wonder if his luck will finally run out.

Rabbit and Scout come to join us. "We think we should take turns scanning the area from now on," Scout says, getting straight to the point.

Rabbit nods enthusiastically. "Not even Damian could say no to that. We should all participate instead of asking for volunteers."

"Some people might not be ready to go out there on their own," I say, even though I don't like the current volunteering system. It leaves Finn too much wiggling space.

"I hope you're not talking about me," Scout says with an offended look on her face. "I survived two months out there before finding you guys. I never get lost. I know every hiding place, every hidden cave and every lost trail."

"We know that, Scout." Finn's arm slides around her shoulders, protective and gentle. "It's a brilliant idea, but you're both needed here more."

"Why am I needed here?" Rabbit challenges Finn.

"Who else could deliver a message if our systems failed? Who could do it faster than you?"

I resist rolling my eyes. Finn could convince a bird the sky isn't blue. Someone really needs to kick his butt.

Our conversation comes to an end when Zoe and Theo announce that they are ready for their presentation.

Damian calls for attention. "The new simulation software allows us all to participate simultaneously."

Zoe's face beams with pride. It's a huge breakthrough—twelve players at once, all of us training together in virtual space. A new chapter for the Saviors, marked by cheers and Biscuit's fresh-baked cookies and the crackle of fire under the stars.

But as I watch Finn's bandaged hand reach for a cookie and think about the alien map hidden away in the Armory, I'm not sure all changes are worth celebrating.

# Chapter 5

I WAKE UP AT dawn, feeling restless. I wrap my blanket around my shoulders to fight the early morning chill and step out of the tent.

Finn is asleep when I slip into his tent on tiptoes. When I poke his shoulder gently, one eye cracks open like a cat disturbed from its nap.

"I need to talk to you," I whisper.

"Everything all right?"

"Nothing's right."

He props himself up on an elbow, fully awake. "What is it?"

I draw in a breath, forcing out the words. "I've been unfair to you, Finn. I'm sorry. I don't know why I reacted the way I did when you came back wounded. I just... I couldn't handle it."

Finn looks at me and laughs. "Wow. Never thought I'd

see the day. You're actually apologizing?"

"What? I apologize all the time," I protest. "I'm constantly messing up, constantly having to say how sorry I am. And you love it every single time."

"Yeah, but those are your escape route apologies. When something makes you uncomfortable, you throw out a *sorry, Finn,* and run. This... this is different."

He reads me like an open book, but I refuse to give him the satisfaction of knowing just how right he is. Instead, I shove him off the bed.

He scrambles back under his blanket, grinning. "Shoo, Tick. Let a wounded man rest. But thank you. Apology accepted."

I'm turning to go when the alarm splits the morning silence. I'm shocked. That system's been in place forever, but it's never once gone off.

Finn jumps to his feet in a flash.

"Hey, take it easy," I say, reaching for his arm. "You're injured, remember?"

"That's cute, but I can manage," he says, patting me on the head like I'm a nervous child.

We sprint to Damian's tent, our designated emergency point. Damian and Theo are hunched over the radar screen. Theo's usually calm face is drawn tight with worry. Others stumble in, drowsy and confused, until the whole group crowds the space.

"All right, we have a situation," Damian says. "Our

radar has picked up unusual activity two miles west. Theo says the movement patterns are erratic and not consistent with any form of intelligent life we know."

That should be reassuring, but it's not. First, sometimes the mindless things are the most dangerous. Second, the radar ignores activity caused by anything under five feet. Theo made sure of that. He had to, really, unless we wanted alerts every time a raccoon wandered past camp.

He spent weeks perfecting that software, muttering to himself while he installed it, determined to create something that would only warn us about real threats: large predators or Sliman. The alien invaders themselves are usually shorter than that, but that hardly matters. They rarely leave their precious plantations, and when they do, their massive Sliman guards tower over them like living fortresses.

We're all thinking it—this has to be connected to that map I found in the forest, somehow. Everything points to one thing. The Sliman are creeping closer to our camp.

"We have two options," Damian says. "Either we send a squad to investigate, or we wait and track the movement on Theo's detection grid, which would be the prudent thing to do for now."

Damian will always choose caution despite his infamous temper. Sometimes I wonder if his hot-headedness is just for show.

We take a quick vote. Damian's cautious approach wins out. We wait.

Theo monitors the activity on the screen of his touch-pad. The tension is palpable in the tent. We struggle to stay patient and calm.

"What do you think it could be?" Rabbit asks Finn, rubbing his hands together.

"I don't know, maybe a wounded animal."

Rabbit's eyes light up. "I could check it out—quick in, quick out. You wouldn't even miss me."

"You heard Damian, we wait," Finn says.

It's one of his most infuriating traits, this unwavering loyalty to the chain of command. He found that phrase, *a soldier's duty*, in some old book in Lost Town and it became his mantra. We've argued about it countless times. But even when he disagrees with Damian, which happens a lot, he will not contradict him, especially in a crisis. It's like his moral compass is set in stone.

Minutes go by slowly, dragging their feet like an eternity.

Theo finally glances up. "The pattern has changed," he says. "This isn't animal behavior. There's purpose to it now... a loose design to the way it's moving. There's intelligence involved and it's getting closer."

Damian's face floods with color, veins bulging at his temples—his telltale sign of frustration. "All these fancy gadgets, what good are they? We've wasted time staring at screens when we should have gone out there and figured it out for ourselves."

"This isn't helping," Finn cuts in. "You wanted to wait. Don't blame Theo, there's no time for pointing fingers."

"I think I might have another solution," Theo says.

"I'm sure you could waste more time at least."

Damian cannot let go of his anger, that's not a surprise, but it's Finn who does something unprecedented—he takes charge.

"Rabbit, Scout, Daphne," Finn commands. "Gear up. You're going with me."

Damian steps in front of Finn. "Since when do you give the orders?"

Finn shrugs. "Since you said we needed eyes out there. I'm just following your command."

Daphne gets between them, pulse gun in hand. "We're ready," she says, nodding toward Rabbit and Scout who wait behind her.

Damian lowers his head, simmering. When he looks up again, his eyes fix on Daphne. "I'm going, too." He turns to Doc. "You're in charge here."

They head out of the camp and my heart sinks. Theo's words echo in my mind. I make my way to where he and Zoe are huddled over a radar screen. "Theo... before... you said you might be able to do something, that you might have another solution. What did you mean?"

Theo hesitates for a moment, then nods decisively. "Come with me."

Zoe and I follow him to his tech lair in the facilities base, which he proudly calls his *hack lab*. It's a cramped space where alien tech, gadgets and devices meet human ingenuity. Here, Theo and Zoe use their magic to repair, improve and reverse-engineer the alien technology.

The room is dark and the air feels damp. Half-finished inventions litter every surface, casting strange shadows in the dim light. Theo's sketches cover the walls—detailed drawings of circuits and devices I can't even name. He turns on a lamp and fires up a gigantic monitor as his fingers fly across the keypad.

I lean in closer, trying to make sense of the scrolling data. "What's the plan?"

"I'm going to mess with their communication satellite control systems." A hint of satisfaction creeps into his voice. "Slimies hate losing their connection to their puppet masters. Usually sends them running back to base."

Zoe's already moving, her hands finding a small device I've seen her working on late into the night. "Where do you need me?"

"Boot up the correlator."

I watch as she activates a strange little touchpad with a specialized antenna that pulses with an orange light. Whatever she's doing must be working, because the code on Theo's monitor starts flowing like water, finding paths through the alien systems.

My hand strays to an old keypad. My fingers tap out random numbers to keep busy. I've barely had time to apologize to Finn, and now he's out there again, running toward danger. I feel useless standing here, but maybe staying out of the way is the best thing I can do.

My touchpad buzzes against my hip. I pull it out of my pocket. Finn's name flashes on the screen.

"What's happening?" I shout into the device. Literally.

"Easy there, Tick. My eardrums," Finn whispers. "Good thing I'm using earphones, or you'd be giving away our position. We've got Sliman scouts. Six of them. They're searching for something. We're tracking their movements. Pass it on."

"Do you think they're looking for the map?"

"Unlikely. Locations don't match."

"Theo's working on cutting their communications," I say, but the connection's already dead. He's offline. A small part of me wonders if he called *me* specifically to make me feel useful, if even in the middle of a crisis, he was thinking about keeping me involved. It would be totally like him.

"Go update Doc, Freya," Theo says without looking up from his screen. He knows how much I hate feeling helpless, and I'm grateful for the task.

I find Doc in headquarters, sitting ramrod straight in Damian's chair. His face is set in that stern expression he wears when he's been given responsibility even if it's temporary.

After I relay Finn's report, Doc immediately pushes out an alert to everyone's touchpads.

"Nya's in position on the observatory tower with her explosive arrows," he informs me. "Biscuit and Tilly are watching the gates. If Tilly spots Sliman coming, we'll have time to reach the tunnel."

"Hey," I protest. "The tunnel? We're the Saviors. We've trained for this. We can't run away from it forever. This is our destiny, to fight back, to make things right. Isn't that why we're here?"

I don't know who is more stunned with my sudden eagerness to engage the enemy—Doc or me.

He chuckles. "You've been spending too much time with Finn."

"Well, someone has to watch out for him," I say with a smile.

"Speaking of Finn, just the other day he said—"

He never gets to finish that sentence. Theo bursts through the door, Zoe on his heels, both their faces flushed.

"It worked!" Zoe says. "We've cut their satellite link. Look, they're already falling back."

Theo thrusts his touchpad at Doc, and I lean in, watching the moving dots on the radar reverse direction. The relief that floods through me is so strong my knees almost buckle. Doc quickly sends the all-clear to Nya, Tilly and Biscuit.

Biscuit beats Tilly and Nya back to headquarters, doubled over and gasping, but still wearing his trademark grin. "So... can we eat now?"

It's his default joke. We've teased him so much about his appetite that he's turned it into his signature line. Even in a crisis, he plays his part perfectly.

The rest of the team gallops in through the main gate moments later, with Damian and Daphne leading the charge.

My eyes fix on Finn bringing up the rear as I notice his uneven gait. The ravine injuries haven't healed yet. He had no business leading a mission. He's not ready. But then again, are any of us truly ready to face Sliman patrols?

The cheers and hugs are cut short when Damian speaks. "What happened today cannot happen again," he snaps at Theo. "If your gadgets can't give us reliable intel fast enough, they're worthless."

Theo's shoulders slump as he stares at the ground. "It won't happen again. I'll figure out what went wrong." I've seen that look on his face before. Damian's approval means everything to him.

I glance at Finn, but his face is carefully neutral. He won't challenge Damian now that the threat is gone. His *soldier's duty* won't allow it. Everyone else is either too young or too reluctant to speak up in Theo's defense.

Fine then. My turn to step up.

"The only reason you all made it back alive is because Theo managed to cut off communications for the Slimies," I say calmly. "He scrambled their satellite frequencies." I look to Zoe for backup. "Right?"

Zoe flinches as if I just poured hot oil on her. Damian's face darkens to a dangerous shade of red as he towers over me. He stares down at me with contempt.

Daphne steps between us. "Give it a rest, Freya. We're safe this time. We'll all learn from this and move forward."

My voice rises despite my efforts to control it. "Why are we attacking the person who made *sure* we'd be safe?"

Finn's hand closes around my arm, steering me firmly toward the door. I struggle against his grip until we're outside.

I wrench free once we reach the tents. "What are you doing? Do you actually agree with him? Are we all just supposed to bow to Damian's temper?"

"Without discipline we've got nothing, Freya."

"You stood up to him earlier!"

"No, I didn't. I reminded him of our priorities in the moment." He sighs as his eyes soften. "Freya, you have things to learn like Daphne said. We all do."

He turns and walks away, leaving me standing alone by the tents. I'm furious and burning with the desire to break something. Hot tears run down my cheeks, and that only infuriates me more.

I feel small. Useless. Powerless. I can't stand it anymore. I need to do something, feel something, feel anything else. I'm not like them—not like Damian with his iron control or Finn with his perfect discipline. Solutions never come to me easily. All I manage to do is go inside Finn's tent and steal his knife.

# Chapter 6

THE SKY IS AN endless expanse of blue as the sun beats down on our compound mercilessly. I'm sitting outside my tent, methodically cleaning and sharpening my knife while keeping one eye on Finn's tent. Doc has ordered him to take the day off to speed up his recovery, and I've decided to do the same, though Finn doesn't know that yet. Just like he doesn't know I'm the reason his knife is missing.

I already regret my momentary lapse in judgment. I'll slip the knife back when he's out on patrol or training, but that doesn't erase my moment of weakness. I'm determined to make things right between Finn and me. We are nothing if we don't learn from our mistakes. And I want to be more than nothing.

The distant sound of metal clashing and banging drifts over from the combat ring, and I find myself relaxing into its familiar rhythm. Strange how the sounds of training for war have become a lullaby, my proof that some things in this upside-down world still make sense.

It's going to be a very hot day. The temperature's already pushing ninety, and it's barely eight in the morning.

I get tired of waiting. I abandon my post to go grab two bottles of chilled water from Theo's cooling system in the main camp. Every day I'm grateful for his engineering genius.

When I return, Finn's awake and examining my knife—the one I left outside my tent like an idiot.

"Good morning," I say with the sincerest smile I can muster.

"Hey." His eyes fall to the bottles in my hands. "Always one step ahead, aren't you?"

"Just trying to prevent our brains from melting." I hold out his water, hyper-aware of my knife in his grip.

"I can't find mine anywhere," he says, handing back my blade. "Must've dropped it in that ravine."

I turn my face the other way, feeling heat crawl up my cheeks that has nothing to do with the weather. "Yeah, you must have." I hate how easily the lie slips out.

There are things I do that make no sense. When you're lost and feel you don't belong, emotions become unreliable. You do things—stupid, desperate things—just to forget that fact. For one crazy moment, it felt like having a piece of him meant I belonged somewhere, but I'm not sure any of that can excuse stealing your best friend's knife.

"No worries, I'll find another," he says, taking a swig of water. He spits it out the side, and I scrunch up my nose. "What?" he says. "Had to rinse the morning out of my mouth."

I'm more disgusted with myself than with him, but I play along. "Must you do that right in front of me?"

"Please. I've seen you do worse, Freya."

I busy myself with my knife, unable to meet his eyes. The blade catches the morning light, throwing accusatory glints.

"When do you start training?" Finn asks.

"I don't. I took the morning off. You know, for some quality time? Isn't that what they used to call it?"

Finn's laugh bursts out of him and despite everything, I find myself laughing too.

His eyes sparkle with amusement. "Been reading books again?"

"Movie, actually." I twist the water bottle in my hands. "Just the first half—I know we're supposed to limit our library time."

"What kind of movie?"

"Family stuff."

"Your favorite."

I don't want to say yes, so I say nothing.

"Well then," Finn continues. "Why don't we go watch

the second half?"

"Yeah. Why not?"

We tell Rabbit where we're headed as insurance against Daphne's inevitable questions. I catch the longing look in Rabbit's eyes. He wants to go too, but right now I need Finn all to myself.

The standing half of the library is our window to all that's been lost. Books, movies, magazines, newspapers and music are all at our disposal. We can watch movies and listen to music on the one ancient computer that Theo managed to repair. Almost everything we know about the world before the aliens came, we learned between these crumbling walls.

At the plantations they drilled us in technology, medicine, physics, math, biology and combat skills, but they never breathed a word about human history, nothing about traditions, about families gathering around dinner tables or children playing in neighborhood streets, nothing about towns or countries. Those things we discovered here, piece by precious piece.

Finn comes alive among history books and files. He never misses a chance to tell me about the American Civil War, the Constitution, the birth of democracy. But nothing gets him going like dinosaurs. He dreams of finding fossils someday and talks about it more often than Rabbit talks about cheetahs.

I'm more fascinated with the way people used to

live—schools bustling with activity, family dinners, movie sets where actors got to slip into different lives. I can't help but wonder what it would be like to have two parents who actually cared for you, who stood in your corner no matter what. But that's a silly dream I'll never voice. Not even to Finn.

His limp is worse today. Each step along the overgrown path makes him favor his right side more. The shrubs press in from both sides, forcing him to twist awkwardly to keep his balance.

I scan the ground until I spot a branch about hip-height. I quickly strip off the leaves before offering it to him.

"Thanks for all the effort, but I don't really need it," he says with a half-smile.

"You don't need it? You can barely walk straight."

"I'm just being careful with the leg, that's all." He sighs as he catches the disappointment on my face and finally accepts the makeshift cane.

"Look who needs it after all," I tease him.

"I'd rather have a walking stick than hear another lecture about how careless I am."

I stick my tongue out at him. "You're lucky you're wounded, or I'd tickle you until you begged for my mercy."

"Don't go giving me any ideas."

I shut up quick. Between the two of us, I'm the one who

can't handle being tickled after all.

Finn sweeps the perimeter with his binoculars before giving me the all-clear. We slip into the library through the crumbling east wall, finding everything exactly as we left it last time.

"I'll grab a book while you queue up your movie," he says. I already know he'll come back with some history tome to thumb through during the film. Usually it drives me crazy, but today my guilt makes me extra generous.

Something in me always settles once we're inside the library. I like to stroll about the silent aisles whose only inhabitants are books and bugs looking to shelter themselves from the heat. I enjoy the feeling of smooth paper on my fingertips as I leaf through book pages. I like studying author photos on dust jackets and trying to piece together the lives they must have led in that vanished world.

I find my movie right where I put it last time and carry it to the computer, crouching down to plug it into the small generator Theo has installed under the floorboards. When I go looking for Finn, he's sitting on the floor, already lost in a book. He barely grunts when I tell him the movie is ready.

"What's so fascinating?" I ask.

"It's funny how people used to communicate back then," he says, carefully returning the book to its shelf.

As I help him up, I catch the title: *Literature's Most Famous Love Stories*.

I bite back a comment but can't help the questioning look that crosses my face when he's not looking.

We settle into chairs in front of the computer monitor. Finn takes an apple out of his pocket.

"Can I have your knife?" he says.

I'm stunned for a second or two before I come to my senses and hand it over. Guilt is an overpowering feeling.

Finn slices the apple while I fast forward the movie to the point I left off last time.

"What have I missed so far?" he asks, passing me my half of the apple.

"Well, there's this family, a mother and four daughters, and they're having a jolly good time. It's Christmas and judging by their fancy dresses, it must be, I don't know, sometime in the early 20th century? There's all this warm family stuff and some sister drama, but in a good way, you know? Though I'm pretty sure something bad's coming, so let's watch."

Twenty minutes later, I turn off the computer and spring out of my chair.

"Freya? What's wrong?"

I shake my head. "Nothing. Everything's fine. We should head back."

His eyes search my face. "It's okay to miss them, Freya. Your mother, your sisters—"

My eyes well up. "Miss them? How could I miss them? I haven't seen them in eleven years."

"Come here," Finn says as he puts his arms around me.

I let myself fold into his embrace, pressing my face against his chest. "You're all I have, Finn, my only family," I whisper. "I never want to fight with you again."

"That'll be the day," he says. I can hear the grin in his voice, feel it rumbling in his chest.

I pull myself together quickly. "Did you put everything back where it belongs?"

He nods, but we still do one last sweep before leaving. Old habits die hard.

The walk back is quiet, but we never have to talk to feel connected. Finn's presence alone makes me feel at home. I'm tempted to confess about the knife, but I don't want to break this moment—just the sun, the breeze, and Finn walking beside me.

My sense of bliss shatters when Finn's hand clamps around my arm, yanking me to the ground.

"What is it?" I whisper, but his sharp hush stops me cold.

He takes out his touchpad and punches in a command. I recognize the sequence—he's activating the sensor in the touchpad. My heart pounds. The device has a very limited range and only picks up signals within a few hundred yards, which means whatever it is he's looking for is close.

*Too close.*

The touchpad flashes confirmation, verifying his fears. There's movement nearby. Maybe a hundred yards out. Finn caught it because he's always prepared, never truly relaxes, never stops watching.

We crawl our way off the path and into the woods, although it might be too late for that. If there are Sliman in the area, chances are they've already marked us.

We press ourselves into the earth, faces inches apart, breathing as shallow as we dare. Only Finn's hand covering mine keeps the panic at bay, his grip reassuring and strong.

We hear heavy footsteps approaching. The sensor light flashes a deep purple. Finn squeezes my hand once before he lets go, reaching for his pulse gun. I do the same. I realize fighting is better than dying.

Three Sliman guards emerge on the path. Their huge figures loom over the landscape menacingly. They move unhurried like they own every inch of ground they cross. I catch glimpses of black cloaks and hoods through the vegetation, hear heavy boots as they hit the ground. I can't see their faces or their insignias, so I can't tell if this is a regular patrol or something else. Something worse maybe.

For a moment, I wonder if we could take them out. With just three of them, we could drop them before they even knew what hit them. One glance at Finn and he reads my mind in an instant. He shakes his head firmly. He's right, of course, but I still wish we could do something useful instead of hiding.

Only when the Sliman have vanished down the path and in the opposite direction from our camp, do we dare to sit up and breathe freely.

"What do you make of this?" I say.

"Something's off. If they were a patrol, they would have detected us. Maybe they're travelling somewhere."

I nod, but... it still doesn't make sense. "Do you think Lost Town is still safe? Damian will probably want to shut down the library visits."

"Yeah, probably. He's not exactly a risk taker," Finn says. "Maybe Theo could install a sensor here to track if more Sliman pass through."

We get up and brush the dust off our clothes. My hands are trembling slightly. Finn notices before I can hide them.

"Calm down, Tick," he says. "We're not in danger any-more."

"I'm not nervous. It's just adrenaline. I made myself ready for battle."

"You sound disappointed."

"Well, what have we been training for? Hiding in bush-es?"

Finn offers me one of his radiant smiles. "Don't be so eager. Battle must have a purpose. It's not just to tickle Tick's fancy."

I shove him, nearly toppling him over.

"What?" he protests, doing his best to look innocent.

I pick up his walking stick and hand it back to him.

"That was your reward for being so clever and condescending in the same breath."

Before I know it, he moves closer. His eyes seem to breathe as they look into mine, alive with something I don't recognize. His lips meet my forehead for a long, brotherly kiss.

RABBIT IS PRACTICALLY QUIVERING with excitement when we get back to the camp.

"Out with it," I command him.

"Scout wants to move to a tent in our part of the camp," he blurts out.

Finn drags a hand down his face. "Oh boy."

"I think it's a perfect idea," I jump in. "The more the merrier."

"Stop egging him on," Finn says.

"Why not? We'll have so much fun."

Even more so because it will annoy Daphne. Watching her face when she finds out will be half the entertainment. It's a win-win situation. Finn will come to appreciate it.

# Chapter 7

WE CREEP FORWARD AT a snail's pace as we enter the three-mile radius of the plantation to avoid being picked up by the invisible web of sensors that blanket the area. Above us, dark clouds roil across the sky—a stroke of luck, since even minor atmospheric interference with the satellites could help mask our presence.

I volunteered the moment Damian announced the mission to map out the plantation closest to the crater, eager to take Finn's place. I owe him this much. He can use all the rest he can get, no matter what he says.

Our small team—Rabbit, Daphne, Tilly, Nya and me—set out yesterday before dawn. The early start gave us enough time to carefully map every step of the way and still carve out time to rest.

Daphne's pacing ahead, leading the mission. I can almost hear Finn's voice. *Promise me you won't give her trouble, Tick.* It's like he lives in my head.

Behind me, Nya mutters something under her breath, probably how long this is taking.

Rabbit is a mix of excitement and worry. Plantation-6, our target, isn't just another mission for him. It's *his* plantation, the place where they trained him, tested him, and broke him in thousands of ways. It's also where he made his first friends, Kicky and Mendy as he calls them. The chances of spotting them among the two thousand children imprisoned there are microscopic. The rational part of him must know that, but hope burns in his eyes anyway.

As we near the plantation, even our breathing feels too loud. We move like ghosts, careful not to disturb even a single blade of grass.

I glance at Rabbit. I can feel the battle inside him—the pull of memories, the weight of what-ifs. I wish I could distract him, tell him some story to pull him out of his thoughts, but all I can do is squeeze his shoulder every now and then.

Rabbit was just eleven when he made his break. The legend of the Saviors had barely reached his ears before he seized his chance—a glitch in the surveillance system, some fight among Sliman guards, and he ran like his life depended on it. Because it did. I was still new to our group of fugitives when Nya spotted him and a team was sent out to bring him in. I couldn't believe an eleven-year-old had managed to escape alone.

Now, two years later, here he is, on a mission to spy on his former prison from the relative safety of the hills. This is our third surveillance operation this summer. We're hoping to map all plantations in the district except twelve through fifteen. No one really knows what happens in those, but the impenetrable layers of security tell their own story. Maybe someday we'll find a fugitive from one of those mysterious compounds. Intel like that would be beyond valuable.

Daphne's raised fist signals that we should halt. She takes out her detection device and scans the frequencies for an opening. A quick nod confirms that we're finally in range. Theo said that once we reached this point, we could safely hijack the satellite control systems, blinding their security tech. We each pull out our touchpads and enter coordinates, so each of us can take control of different satellite functions.

"All right," Daphne whispers, "we have twenty minutes before the aliens detect the interference. Let's make them count."

Her powers of intellectual manipulation might not work on me, but she's right about the main part. We need to get to the hilltop and document everything we can.

We move faster now that we have some control, though conversation stays minimal. We've done enough missions together to know each other's patterns. Rabbit retreats into himself when focused, Nya barely ever talks unless she has to, and Daphne... well, she's busy savoring her leadership role—her personal addiction and one true passion. That leaves Tilly humming a quiet tune under her breath.

We reach our vantage point in three minutes. Seventeen more minutes of relative safety left. We could probably stretch it another five or six, but why take the chance? Better to stay invisible, under the radar, seen by none, remembered by none.

The plantation sprawls below us, at least half its facilities and other utilitarian buildings laid bare to our view. Through our high-powered binoculars, every detail springs into sharp focus: a scattered leaf, a fly perched on a Sliman guard's helmet, a small dent in a magnetic bow. I glance at Tilly, wondering if she even needs the tech—her vision's already superhuman.

I catalog each structure while Daphne photographs them: the stark HQ building, the prison-like dorms, the sterile labs, the industrial kitchens, the communal lavatories, the training arena where they break bodies and spirits, the simulators that reshape minds, the controlled library, the heavily guarded armory. The layout mirrors the other plantations we've surveyed, a blueprint copied and pasted across the district.

A group of children exits the simulation chambers. They walk in perfect formation with their heads slightly bowed, wearing those brown uniforms I remember so well, hair so short it might as well have been shaven off. The sight is so familiar that it sends a pang through my heart, yanking me back in time.

I was seven when they brought me to Plantation-8. I thought my world had ended that day. I didn't know I would find Finn there, but even if I'd known, it wouldn't have been much of a consolation. Everything felt menacing and cold, like a walk on cracking ice with the gaping mouth of chaos underneath.

They stripped away every piece of my identity. They took my clothes away and replaced them with that dreadful brown uniform. They cut off my hair and forced me to swallow a bunch of pills. They probed my throat, nose and ears. They tested my reflexes and my pain threshold with small electric shocks. They drilled and capped my teeth. They jabbed me with needles and scanned every inch of my body like I was livestock.

When they finished, they classified me as 8-78349Z32 and sent me off to report to my dorm. There, they burned away my old identification mark and branded the new number into my neck.

"This is your name now," they said, as if seven years of being a human child meant nothing.

The whole time, I was drowning inside, felt like I was dying. I ached for my baby sisters, for my mother, that hollow-eyed, silent woman who'd already been stripped of everything but her ability to breed.

I never knew who she'd been before, when she was a young girl like me, before they turned her into a vessel. Sometimes I imagine her with fire in her eyes instead of that vacant stare, with dreams instead of emptiness.

Rabbit's sudden poke startles me so badly I drop my touchpad.

"Have you ever seen a female alien? Or a female Sliman?" he says.

The image of a Sliman in a dress is so absurd that I choke on my own laughter.

"Of course not," Daphne intervenes. "Nobody has. Why ask questions we all know the answers to?"

"He was talking to me," I remind her. "We like to talk about things. Like friends do."

"What I'm trying to say," Rabbit presses on, "is that the aliens must keep their females somewhere else, maybe on their planet, maybe in some secret place on Earth. What if the females are weaker, more vulnerable? Maybe we can end this war if we find them. No more ladies, no more alien babies."

"We don't have time for fantasies," Daphne says, rolling her eyes.

"But what if he's onto something?" Tilly joins in, her voice animated. "What if that's the key, the female counterparts? Or, what if there's only one female, a super alien, like a queen bee? Find the queen, destroy the whole colony." Her face is beaming with hope.

"You guys are reaching," Daphne says. She shakes her head and fixes her attention back on her camera.

"She's right. No shortcuts. We kill them all, one by one," Nya whispers in her matter-of-fact voice. Nya doesn't say much, but she likes to have the last word.

"Who said anything about shortcuts?" Tilly says.

Daphne reaches for her pulse gun. "Quiet, all of you, something's wrong."

Tilly's body tenses as her enhanced senses scan for danger. "What is it?"

"Part of our shield is down, creating white noise in the satellite transmission. There's some odd movement down there, look!"

A Sliman patrol materializes by the armory, forming up with terrifying speed and precision.

"They're on to us," Daphne says. "Who's monitoring the blue shield interface?"

My heart stops. My touchpad screen has gone dark—must have shut off when I dropped it. Daphne gives me the coldest glare I've seen, and that includes the Director at Plantation-8.

I fumble to restart my touchpad, but the damage is done. We need to move—now. We have minutes, maybe just seconds, before they pinpoint our location. My mind races with guilt and self-recrimination. How did I miss my touchpad going dark? Where was my head? This kind of mistake gets people killed, and everyone knows it, including me.

We sprint down the slope for dear life, struggling to match Rabbit's pace. If we can reach the designated safe spot on time, we'll need to slow to a crawl. Hopefully, that will convince the sensors that they detected a system glitch.

I realize that Tilly is falling behind. Daphne and I lock eyes for a split second, reading each other's minds. We sprint back, each grabbing one of Tilly's arms. Her ankle's clearly injured, but there's no time for gentle treatment. We half-drag, half-carry her until we hit Theo's safe zone.

We come to a stop, exchanging silent nods. No speaking, no sudden movements until we're beyond the plantation's surveillance range. The return journey stretches endlessly. Tilly's face contorts with each step, but she doesn't make a sound. Rabbit hovers by her side, worried.

Daphne's expression is unreadable, but I'm sure she's furious. She doesn't say a word until we stumble back into camp, exhausted and ragged. Rabbit races ahead to fetch Doc, so he can take care of Tilly's swollen foot. They return moments later with a stretcher.

As Nya and I move to follow them, I hear Daphne's voice.

"Not so fast, Freya. Come with me."

I guess I knew this was coming. Daphne would never let me off the hook, especially for such a serious mistake.

Damian waits at his desk, disappointment written all over his face. I didn't expect Daphne to cover for me, but I'm a bit surprised she has already filled him in. She acts like an obedient puppy around him, always eager to please him, and my humiliation is probably an added bonus.

"Do you realize you've jeopardized the very existence of the Saviors?" Damian says in a calm voice that's somehow worse than anger.

I nod. I know that he's right.

"Why volunteer when you're clearly not ready?" he continues.

"That's obvious to everyone but Freya herself," Daphne says, twisting the knife.

Damian remains maddeningly calm. "You're confined to camp until further notice. Train. Make yourself useful. Learn. No more missions or running off with Finn. You're nothing but a distraction to him."

I bite my tongue until I taste blood. I have about a thousand things I want to say to defend myself, but I think of Finn and his lessons in restraint. I still have his knife, a reminder that I have lied to him, that I'm different. I fight back the urge to speak. It always ends badly. So, I listen. I nod. I am utterly and perfectly humiliated.

I find Finn with Rabbit, both wearing identical expressions of concern and curiosity. I recount everything, hating how my voice shakes despite my best efforts to remain strong.

"Let me get this straight, you just stood there and said nothing?" Finn asks me.

"Yeah. That's what I said."

"Why?"

Is he serious? "You've always told me to respect authority."

"I said don't challenge Damian publicly or resort to shouting as an argument. But you need to defend yourself, Tick. Present the facts. Rabbit told me he accidentally bumped you. Why didn't you explain that? Why take full blame for an accident?"

"Because it *was* negligence on my part. And because I'm not going to drag Rabbit into my mess. And—" I swallow hard. "Because I'm tired of disappointing you."

"I will explain to Red," Rabbit offers.

"You'll do no such thing," I say. "I'll do what I have to do. I'll train. I'll even try to learn as Damian suggested. Just, both of you, let me deal with this my own way."

Finn surprises me with a grin. He regards me with something new in his eyes. He leans in for a hug. "I understand, Tick. I might even be a little proud of you, but you should choose your battles more wisely in the future."

In my tent, I sink onto my bed. All the fatigue of the previous days weighs me down. I meant what I said about learning, about improving. I need to. But knowledge comes at a huge price in our world, and I can't help but wonder if it will all be worthwhile in the end.

# Chapter 8

THERE'S A LOT TO be said about someone who runs from responsibility, and none of it is good. I don't want to be that kind of person. I refuse to be the one Savior who couldn't put the common good above herself.

I sit in the Armory, between Tilly and Scout, waiting for the weekly meeting to begin. I don't expect any unpleasant surprises today—I know what's on the agenda—but that doesn't stop my fingers from drumming against my thigh.

"The forest is where the real training happens," Scout says. "The combat ring is too... unexciting. Nothing to track, nothing to hunt."

Tilly snorts. "Yeah, except for those killer bees that nearly took us out last time. Or did you forget about that little *excitement*?"

Scout waves her hand dismissively. "What are the odds

of that happening twice? A few bees are hardly a thing to worry about."

"Those hives haven't exactly packed up and moved," Tilly points out.

"It doesn't matter if they're still there," I cut in. "We know where they are now and we won't bother them."

"Unless there are more hives we don't know about."

Scout leans forward. "Come on, Tilly! You're not afraid of a few buzzing insects, are you? We're fighting for humanity's survival. We need to get beyond these walls more, not less."

The debate dies down as the heavy Armory door creaks open and Damian walks into the room with Daphne. Zoe, our designated note-taker today, settles next to Damian, while Daphne takes her place at his other side.

After announcing the day's agenda, Daphne yields to Damian. He rises slowly, deliberately, and crosses the room to the whiteboard. We turn our heads to track him moving. The red marker squeaks against the board as he draws an electrical circuit. Then he erases a tiny section of the voltage loop.

"You take away the smallest particle and the circuit fails," he says. He turns to face us, and his eyes find mine with laser precision. "There's been too much of that lately. Freya and Theo have jeopardized our entire existence through negligence or haste on two occasions. I think we deserve to hear how they plan to improve attention to mission detail and to ensure our survival isn't compromised by such carelessness in the future."

I know I've promised myself and Finn that I'll try to be more of a team player, but if Damian keeps pushing me like this, I won't be responsible for what comes out of my mouth. He can drag me through the mud all he wants, but Theo? The way I remember it, Theo saved our lives the other day.

Some *negligence* indeed!

"I know I'm asking for a lot. Our lives are far from easy, but we are free and I hope we can stay that way," Damian says, pausing for effect. "We're in this together. We must have each other's backs."

His hand rises, index finger pointing at me with all the authority of a judge passing sentence. The gesture draws all eyes in the room. I have no choice. I walk slowly up to the whiteboard, having no idea what the heck I'm going to say once I'm there that won't make this worse.

"I thought I'd give you a chance to speak for yourself," Damian says, staring intensely at me with a furrowed brow.

I feel like I could kill him. Well, at the very least smack that smug look off his face and introduce him to the nearest black hole. It must be nice living up there on his moral high ground, raining judgment down on those of us just trying to do our best in an impossible situation.

*Say something, quick!*

"I don't know what you expect me to say, Damian. Yes, there was an accident during the mission at Plantation-6. I dropped my touchpad and it went into auto-shutdown. I don't plan to make a habit of it. No need to worry about this kind of thing repeating." I lift my chin, meeting his gaze. "And Theo, he saved the entire camp. He doesn't need to explain anything."

Damian's face flushes red. "Can you, for once, stick to the part that's relevant to you? It's always an accident with you, isn't it?"

The fight drains from me. He's right about one thing—my mental lapse put lives at risk. I can't defend that, and trying will only make me look like I'm ducking responsibility. My eyes find Finn's across the room, searching for guidance, for any hint of what I'm supposed to do. His expression is unreadable, a brick wall where I need a window.

I decide to go with my instinct.

"I was wrong. I screwed up. I'm sorry. We all know this. If you needed me to say it, I said it. Now what?" The room stays deathly silent. Something dark claws its way up my throat. "We are all accidents, Damian, if I must state the obvious. We were born into an enslaved world, meant to serve until we were killed or lobotomized."

I wait for Finn to cut me off, to pull me back from this edge, but I sense he's given up on me. Fine, let the truth shine. "Sooner or later, we'll face our real test. Not these little accidents and mishaps. Failure then will mean death or worse. I have no intention of failing when that day comes. What choice do I have but to believe in myself?"

There's a short pause, then Rabbit claps to show his support. Scout joins in, but the rebellion ends there, suffocated by the weight of judgment in Damian's eyes.

That stare is so unwavering, I think it might burn holes through my skull.

"You always sound good, Freya, like you have a crusade you're leading," he says. "But our only crusade right now is staying alive. You were tested, truly tested, and you failed; and now you want to make that everyone's fault but your own." He shakes his head, frustrated. "Until your attitude changes, you'll keep failing these tests. Nothing you've said shows me you're ready for real responsibility, or that your companions can trust you with their lives."

"I don't know what you want me to say. That I'll be more careful?"

"It's not about what I want you to say, it's about what you want. About what you're willing to do to make sure you're solid in every moment that matters. We'll continue to wait for you, but not forever."

His final words sting and make it hard to breathe. His conversation with Theo fades to background noise—something about an apology, promises to work harder to improve device performance, to react faster and more efficiently. Then I stop listening altogether.

FINN WALKS ME TO the simulators for my scheduled session. "For what it's worth, I agree with some of what you said."

"Some but not all, right?" The bitterness in my voice surprises even me.

"Freya, I will talk to Damian."

"Let it go, Finn. Damian's had enough of you defending me."

He takes my hand. "I believe in you," he says. "Never forget that."

I leave him standing outside the simulators. It's not my turn yet, so I wait, thinking about the breeding village again and the family I left behind.

I have no proof that my mother loved us. The aliens did their best to strip away everything that made her human—her intelligence, her emotions, her spirit. But I believe love survived somewhere deep inside her, even if she never found a way to show it. Sometimes, I think I remember moments, fleeting touches, looks that meant more than they seemed. Or maybe that's just what I need to believe.

My chest aches thinking of her alone now with all her

children gone. They'll have reassigned her as a servant, a cook for the Sliman or a cleaner for the village labs. No one's ever seen a human past sixty, but she's only forty now. They will let her work, let her exist in that half-life they've created for her.

I wish I could see her again, just once. I wish I could hug her and tell her I love her, promise her she'll always be in my heart and that one day I'll save her, so she can live on even when she goes gray like the old humans.

Gosh, I'm as bad as Rabbit with these daydreams. My turn comes up for the simulation, and I welcome the chance to shut out all thoughts and blow things to pieces.

When I return to my tent, I find Finn waiting for me outside.

"Don't you have anything better to do than hide in shadows?" I tease, but then I see what he's holding—the knife I stole from him.

"Want to explain how my knife ended up under your bed?"

"Want to explain why you were searching my tent?" I counter, as my defensive instincts kick in.

"Daphne found three mattresses in a basement in Lost Town, still wrapped. Yours is falling apart, so I thought ..." His voice trails off, but his eyes won't leave mine. "I wanted to surprise you."

I nod, not knowing what to say.

"Why did you take my knife, Freya? Why did you hide

it? You know I need this knife. What were you trying to prove?"

I shrug. "I don't know, I was angry when I took it. I've been trying to give it back."

He tries to hand his knife to me, but I don't take it. "See, that's all it takes to give it back. It hardly takes any trying at all."

"Yeah, and have you mad at me once again."

"Me? Mad at you? What?" I seem to have hit a nerve. "You're the one who's always mad at me. Everything I do annoys you." He exhales and tries to calm down. "Why didn't you give the knife back when I told you I lost it?"

"I was going to put it back eventually."

He peers into my eyes, coldly.

"Come on, Finn," I say as I lose my nerve. "Don't look at me like that. Please."

"Eventually is not an option. One day hesitation will be our undoing. Hesitation is death out there." Another careful breath. "Freya, your worst enemy, your only enemy, is yourself. Damian's right. I can't help you. Only you can."

When he turns away, I feel suddenly alone, orphaned. I want to run after him and beg for his forgiveness, but that's my whole problem. I react too fast, too strong, too selfishly. Maybe tomorrow he'll hate me less. He can't just stop caring for me, can he? Not after all these years.

Inside the tent, the new mattress waits on the bed like

an accusation. I sit on it and despite everything, my body relaxes into its perfect balance of firm support and gentle comfort. The best mattress I've ever had. It feels like a goodbye gift.

No, Finn will understand. And if he doesn't, I'll make him understand. Everything will go back to normal. We're connected, always have been. This time, I'll be the friend he deserves. The friend everyone deserves.

That's what he wants, and I can never imagine a life without Finn.

# Chapter 9

I'M NOT EXACTLY A fan of cleaning days, but today I'm almost relieved it's my turn. Maybe mopping and sweeping will keep me from mulling over the same stuff in an endless loop. It helps that Tilly is on duty too. Her constant chatter and stubborn cheerfulness, even with her foot bandaged, are exactly what I need.

We've just finished the worst part, cleaning the bathrooms. With my mood in shambles and my focus shot, it would've been pure torture if not for Tilly. Somehow, she makes even this miserable chore feel a little lighter.

We head to the kitchen, which is at least a step up from the bathrooms. We start clearing glasses and plates from the tables. It's hard to believe this used to be a lab before we swept in and took over. Two weeks of backbreaking work, scrubbing out chemical stains, tearing down shelves of glassware, transformed it into a place where food could be prepared. Two massive ovens, once used for chemical reactions, now serve a far nobler purpose—feeding us, day in and day out.

Biscuit, without a doubt, is the most accomplished cook among us. He can make even the simplest ingredients taste like a feast. Theo, on the other hand, is notorious for his questionable experiments in the kitchen, which often end in burnt pans and strange smells. I rank somewhere in the middle alongside Tilly, whose enthusiasm usually compensates for her lack of culinary prowess.

Tilly glances at me as she stacks plates. "Better than scrubbing toilets, right?" she says, nudging me lightly with her elbow.

I can't help but smile. "By a mile."

The kitchen is functional, even if it's far from perfect. Metal counters and cupboards line the walls, two long tables with six mismatched chairs each sit at the center, and a large, broken clock hangs on a wall, permanently stuck at 3:47. On the opposite wall, a picture of a rooster rescued from a demolished house in Lost Town adds an odd touch of personality to the room. It's practically the only thing from that house that survived intact, as if protected by some strange magic.

"Tilly, you take the counters. I'll handle the ovens," I say, grabbing a cloth and some soap. It's only fair—her ankle's still swollen, and my only injury is my bruised pride.

She limps slightly as she moves to the counters. "Deal."

I focus on wiping the ovens, one of which seems determined to keep its layer of grease like a badge of honor. Tilly gasps suddenly. She reaches behind the mixer and emerges with a bowl of half-eaten dough.

"I know who's been here," she says, and we both exclaim in unison, "Biscuit!"

The laughter that follows breaks through the monotony of our tasks. It's not the first time we've found Biscuit's signature in the most predictable place.

When Biscuit got his name, it wasn't through the usual book method, but no one can deny how perfectly it suits him.

It happened during a walk along a creek. The water was clear, the sunlight dancing on its surface, when Rabbit pointed to some small, round things floating downstream. "What's that?" he asked, squinting.

Biscuit's eyes turned gooey. "It looks like biscuits to me."

We all exchanged glances, holding back laughter, realizing his mistake.

Damian was the one who said it. "It's moose turds, you nincompoop."

Rabbit and Scout fell to the ground, clutching their stomachs. Even Damian cracked a rare grin, maybe even chuckled.

But it was Biscuit's face that undid me. The way he kept staring at those floating droppings, hoping we were all wrong. What else could I do? I found myself on the ground with the others, laughing so hard tears blurred my vision.

That's how a boy named Harry had his name changed to Biscuit.

"It's a wonder he doesn't weigh two hundred pounds by now," Tilly says, wiping down the counter.

I smile, picturing Biscuit in one of his eating marathons. The truth is, he burns calories faster than Rabbit can cover a mile. All that food? It just fuels his relentless workouts.

"We all have our regrettable habits," I say with a shrug. "Biscuit's aren't that bad and he gets away with them."

"There's not a single thing bad about him. He's thoughtful, gentle, funny... and his laugh? No one laughs like Biscuit."

"Except maybe you," I tease her.

She scrunches up her face, clearly flustered. Tilly likes Biscuit. It's written all over her.

"He's better than me at almost everything—physical stuff, intellectual stuff. You name it," she says.

"Wait, are we still talking about Biscuit here? Am I missing something?"

"What do you mean?"

"I mean, Biscuit isn't better than you. You both have

your strengths, sure, but yours? They are exceptional. As Doc once put it, you have bionic eyes and ears. Nobody can beat that."

Tilly blushes. "Well, I wasn't exactly talking about the special abilities the aliens implanted in us." She pauses to look at me. "Although, Biscuit's nose *could* be bionic."

"A bionic nose? What good would that be?"

"I don't know, but have you seen how good he is at martial arts practice lately? He keeps getting better."

"Okay, okay, we've established that Biscuit is amazing." Tilly blushes more now, so I change the subject. "But seriously, everyone is exceptional in their own way. Like you said, for some reason, the aliens made us this way."

*Except me.*

"But, Freya, we're more than their experiments. Don't say it so coldly. Our hearts and minds, those are still ours."

I nod, her words striking a chord. "You're right, Tilly. Of course, you are. And you know what? The most exceptional thing about the Saviors isn't what they did to us. It's that we've got each other's backs."

She runs her hand across the counter. "Yeah, I never got a chance to properly thank you, you know, for coming back for me up in the hills, you and Daphne."

Regret surfaces again. My daydreaming was the reason she got hurt in the first place. It could have cost Tilly her freedom or worse. "You don't have to thank me. You would have done the same," I say sheepishly. "That's what we do. We have each other's backs, remember?"

Tilly looks up at me. "Still... thanks."

I smile, placing a hand on her shoulder. "Always, Tilly."

"Biscuit says we are like *The Three Musketeers*. One for all and all for one."

I chuckle. "Probably easier to make three as one than twelve as one."

"*The Three Musketeers* are actually four," she informs me.

"Is that a book he's read?"

"Yes, Biscuit made me read it too. He said it was important."

"I'll put it on my reading list."

We get back to work. My sponge scrapes against the metal oven walls and Tilly's cloth squeaks across tables. When she goes quiet, really quiet, I know something's brewing. Tilly's thoughts are like thunderstorms. They build and build until they break.

"Freya?"

"What is it?"

She hesitates for a second. "Do you think there's such a thing as love?"

I pause, brush stuck mid-scrub, searching for the right answer. "Of course, there is. We love each other, don't we?"

She stops her work, turning to face me. Her expression is dead serious. "Not that kind. I mean, love like we read in the novels. Romeo and Juliet kind of love."

It finally hits me. "Oh, Tilly. Does Biscuit know?"

"Know what?"

"That you love him."

"I don't! That's not why I'm asking." She spins away, attacking the table with renewed vigor.

"Well, if that's not it, then no, I don't believe in romantic love. Not in our world. There's no time for that. No point."

I think I've said the right thing. After all, we're all so new to this life, this strange, unshackled autonomy. It would be silly to believe we can truly control our futures when there's an alien invasion bearing down on Earth. Every sunset could be our last for all we know.

"But don't you think... maybe it could make everything feel less empty? Like, if you found someone who understood you, who made it all feel—" She hesitates. "Better?"

"Maybe. But that's a big *if*, Tilly. Our world doesn't leave much room for better."

"You really don't believe in it?"

I shrug. "I believe in us. That's enough for me."

But Tilly isn't done. She steps closer with new determination. "Freya, how can you say that? What about you and Finn?"

I blink, caught off guard. "Finn and me? You can't be serious."

"Why not? You're always sneaking off together. You

always support him, and he always supports you. Just like in the books."

"Tilly, Finn and I are friends. Very good, close friends. At least we were, until I messed everything up."

Her eyebrows shoot up. "What happened?"

"Let's just say it might take him a while before he forgives me."

Her eyes light up with that familiar mischievous glint that usually means trouble. "I'll believe you if you say so, but just so you know, everyone thinks differently."

*Okay, what?*

"Everyone? Who's everyone?"

"Everyone is everyone. Well, except maybe Damian. He probably doesn't think about stuff like that. But definitely Biscuit, Rabbit and Scout. Zoe and Nya, too. Girls notice things."

"You're all insane. Quit talking about me behind my back."

"We've only discussed it once or twice, honestly," Tilly says, a bit hurt by my reaction. "And it really wasn't focused on Finn and you. We were just talking about... what love really is. And why people used to think about it so much before the invasion."

These kinds of thoughts have probably crossed all our minds. But they are counterproductive meanderings, distractions we can't afford. Our lives are hard enough as it is.

"I'm sorry, Tilly," I mutter. "I didn't mean to bite your head off."

Tilly glances up, her grin slowly returning. "It's okay. You're just sensitive about Finn."

I groan. "Tilly—"

A light breeze sweeps through the kitchen as Daphne strides in and yanks open the fridge door. She rummages through jars and bottles but can't find what she's looking for.

She turns to us. "Is there no lemonade left?"

"I don't know," Tilly says.

I point to the fruit basket on the counter. "There are lemons right there. Why don't you make some fresh lemonade? I could use a glass after all this scrubbing."

Daphne's response is to slam the fridge door shut and storm out of the kitchen. Typical.

Tilly sighs. "Now, Daphne is like an open book even though she tries so hard not to be. She only has eyes for Damian, but he seems completely clueless. It's obvious she's *in love* with him. Even you can see it, right? Isn't it romantic?"

I blink at her, dumbfounded. *Daphne? Romantic?* The thought is so absurd it takes a moment to process. "Tilly, where do you even get these ideas? Daphne. *In love.* Re-ally?"

Tilly gives me an exasperated look. "She acts all tough, but the way she looks at him? Come on, Freya."

"Daphne likes Damian, sure. She also knows which side of his temper she wants to be on. That's not love. You need a heart for that, don't you?"

Tilly swats my arm with her cleaning cloth. "That's harsh."

It probably is, but the idea of Daphne, of all people, being head-over-heels for Damian is too ridiculous to take seriously. It might even top the nonsense they've been spinning about Finn and me.

Obviously, we all have too much time on our hands.

❖

DAPHNE CATCHES UP WITH me on my way to the showers. I immediately dread her sense of urgency. "Whatever it is, can it wait?" I say without slowing down. "I'm feeling grimy after all that cleaning. I need to hit the shower."

"Relax, I'm not here to lecture you. I just want to talk."

I almost stumble. Daphne wants to talk to me. I would have been less surprised if she sprouted wings and flew away. For better or worse, she's managed to grab my attention. Part of me wants to play nice, to put our silly differences aside.

"It's safe to say that you hate Damian, am I right?" she says with a disarming smile.

It takes a moment for her words to register, and when they do, I blink in confusion. "Hate him? Of course, I don't hate him. I don't hate anyone. At least, no one human."

"Not even me?"

"Daphne, where is this going? I really just want to shower."

She steps in front of me, places both hands on my shoulders and locks her eyes with mine. "I noticed you didn't answer the question," she says.

"I don't hate you, Daphne."

"That's nice to know. Really. Maybe now you know it, too."

I nod, unsure why I feel compelled to agree with everything she says. I can't look away. Her eyes shine like two blue stones in the night. I feel like a stunned deer staring at bright lights. A strange haze clouds my thoughts.

"Your dislike of me comes only from my association with the person you truly hate," she goes on. "The person who really stands between you and your self-esteem. Damian."

I almost nod again when something inside me snaps to attention. The haze lifts and I put two and two together. Daphne's spell is broken. I sweep her hands off my shoulders and take a step back. "What are you doing? You're not allowed to hypnotize me without my consent! We have rules about this!"

She laughs my protests off, unbothered. "It's just a joke, Freya. I didn't actually think you'd fall for it."

"A joke? Do you see me laughing?"

She shakes her head with mock disapproval. "You're too serious. That's the whole problem with you. Lighten up, Freya. Life's too short."

She strolls away while I stand frozen, trying to piece myself back together after the strange confusion she's left in her wake. Her mind games have reached a whole new level.

Of all the things she has pulled on me, this must have been the strangest.

# Chapter 10

THE DAY IS BRILLIANT, the kind that feels like a rare gift. A soft breeze blows from the north, jostling leaves and filling lungs with crisp air. A welcome reprieve after days of relentless heat, and perfect conditions for a training session in the forest.

For the first time in a while, the camp will be empty and unguarded. The only thing standing between us and whatever lurks in the shadows is Theo's sensor grid, ready to alert us if anything unusual happens while we're gone.

Our training site is a small clearing deep in the woods, about two miles south of camp, past the hills. It's secluded, surrounded by towering trees that shield us from the sun and prying eyes.

We split our time between group drills and individual training—martial arts, target shooting, sword fighting—preparing for a future none of us want to face.

Finn has been nice to me all morning. *Too* nice. He showed me how to secure rope loops around branches and kept an eye on me during fighting practice, offering tips when necessary, but he's keeping his distance in ways that only I would notice. It's the subtle way his gaze slides past mine, the careful space he maintains between us. And it breaks my heart.

No matter how many times I apologize, he will not fully forgive me. With Finn, forgiveness has to be earned through action, through proof that I'm actually changing.

It's always been like that with him. Even back at Plantation-8, he held himself and everyone else to impossibly high standards as far as honesty. "Without trust," he'd say, "we don't have anything."

Life at Plantation-8 was brutal… exhausting. It left you feeling alone and hollow, like a machine forced to keep running on empty. Our schedules were packed so tightly that we barely had time to breathe, let alone think about what might come next. In a way, it was a blessing in disguise. Thinking too much might have broken us completely.

We weren't allowed to talk except during meals and the half-hour break before the lights went out. Even then, we had to speak in low voices and one at a time. The alien directors despised disorder and noise, and the Sliman guards enforced their rules with merciless efficiency.

But Finn wasn't one to follow rules blindly. He raised his voice one day in the dining hall during our brief break. He didn't sound angry but defiant and bold in a way none of us dared to be. He questioned why the aliens kept us alive, why they trained us, why they bothered to teach us to read and write, and why they let us socialize and develop distinct personalities.

It didn't take long for two Sliman guards to walk into the dining hall. They ordered Finn to stand up. When they told him to repeat what he'd said, Finn didn't hesitate. He stood tall, his face calm, and repeated every word without flinching, without altering a syllable.

The Sliman guards struck Finn with a taser. The charge sent him crumpling to his knees. He was only twelve, but at the plantations, age meant nothing. We had all grown into a forced adulthood, our edges had been hardened. We learned early that survival meant relying only on ourselves.

Finn was taken away that day and didn't return until the following week. Those seven days were agony. I feared he would be dead or shipped to another plantation. My body ached with despair, and my soul was inconsolable. My eleven-year-old self couldn't articulate then what was in my heart, but now I can: I loved Finn with a fierce desperation that defied every rule, every regulation imposed on us. I needed him like I needed air.

When Finn came back, he was thinner and ghost-pale.

He had endured electroshocks, he had been starved for five days and then pumped full with nutrients and medications to keep him alive. He went through hell, but he did not back down. Finn didn't lie then, and he won't lie now no matter how much the truth can hurt.

I shake my head to force the memories away. *Focus.* I scan the area around me, searching for the least conspicuous way to slip away from the group. Before I can take a step, Daphne barrels into me, knocking me flat on the ground. She loses her balance and tumbles down beside me, her breathing fast and loud in my left ear. Our limbs get tangled, and for a moment, I can only blink at her in stunned confusion.

"What are you—" I start, but then she points to a small dark shape scuttling across the dirt a few feet away before disappearing under a rock.

"A scorpion," she says, getting to her feet and brushing herself off. Without another word, she walks away at a brisk pace.

I stay on the ground, watching her retreating figure. Something nags at me. Did she really see that scorpion from a hundred yards away? Is she really superhuman like she's been claiming? Or is this another one of her mind games?

If I'm honest, Daphne wouldn't irritate me half as much if I hadn't started pushing her buttons from day one. Well, maybe not *exactly* day one. At first, I was too grateful to her and Damian for their part in my liberation to cause any trouble. But things changed quickly once Damian was voted leader of the Saviors. Daphne immediately positioned herself as his confidant, his right hand, and his self-appointed second-in-command.

It's late afternoon by the time we decide to head back to camp. We take off in pairs, keeping our formation tight: Rabbit and Scout at the head, Damian and Daphne right behind them, Theo and Zoe covering the back. I walk next to Tilly, while Finn trails several feet behind us with Biscuit. As part of the exercise, we remain silent and alert, scanning the forest for any sign of danger.

Tilly struggles with the silence part. Her hand keeps finding mine, squeezing, while she fidgets with her hair and the hem of her shirt. I can almost feel the words bubbling up inside her, barely held back until we reach the camp.

She finally gives in, leaning close to whisper, "Guess who was having a secret conversation behind the bushes earlier."

"Define secret," I say under my breath, keeping my eyes on the path ahead.

"You know, the kind where people talk about things they don't want anyone else to hear."

I sigh. "Everyone's entitled to their privacy, Tilly. Spying on people isn't exactly building trust."

"Freya, please. I wasn't spying. I heard maybe two

sentences before I realized and left."

"Then why are you telling me?"

"Because it was Finn—"

Damian's hand shoots up. "Get down!"

We drop to the ground, forming a tight defensive circle. My heart pounds against the dirt as I glance around.

Rabbit jumps into the middle of the circle, his face ashen. "We're in trouble," he chokes out.

"Details, Rabbit," Damian says.

Rabbit nods, catching his breath. "I got eyes on the camp from the overlook. Someone—something—tore through it like a hurricane. The area around the supply building and the kitchen is trashed. Plants are bent and broken, tents pulled down, scattered food everywhere."

"Off the path," Damian orders. "Into the trees. Now."

We scramble off the trail, taking cover among the dense foliage. I press my back against the rough bark of a tree, my mind racing.

Finn's voice comes from somewhere to my left. "What's our play?"

Damian grabs Rabbit's arm. "Rabbit and I will go in first to evaluate the situation."

"I'm going too," Daphne says, pulling out her pulse gun.

Finn steps forward. "Count me in."

Damian shakes his head. "No, you stay here and take care of the group. Keep them safe."

Finn opens his mouth to argue, but the look Damian gives him shuts him down before he starts.

"Stay out of sight," Damian tells us. "We'll be back as soon as we know what's going on."

He and Rabbit disappear into the trees. The rest of us crouch in the bushes to wait. No one speaks. The silence is heavy, charged like the air after a sudden explosion.

Then Finn does something I never expected. He wraps his arm around Daphne's shoulders, pulling her close. "Damian and Rabbit will be back soon," he says. "Everything's going to be okay."

Daphne leans into him, resting her head against his shoulder like she belongs there. It only lasts a moment, but it's enough to make my stomach twist.

My mind snaps back to Tilly's unfinished sentence before Damian raised the alarm. Was this what she overheard? Finn and Daphne talking in secret? The thought feels wrong somehow. Since when are they so close? What could they possibly have to talk about?

I glance at Tilly, but she's huddled next to Biscuit, nervously pulling her sleeves over her fingers. She looks small and more scared than I've ever seen her. My questions will have to wait, if I even ask them at all. What right do I have to expect answers? What do I care what Finn or anyone else does? We're all free now, aren't we? Free to choose, free to have secrets, free to hurt each other in whole new ways.

Evening creeps in around us—the forest grows darker, easier to hide in. I close my eyes and focus on the cool breeze brushing against my face, trying to ground myself in its refreshing touch.

"How are you holding up?" Finn's voice beside me makes me jump. His hand finds mine in the darkness, warm, familiar, and suddenly strange. "Hey, it's me."

He sits down next to me, close but not close enough. I wish he'd hold me like he did Daphne, wrap his arm around my shoulders and make everything right between us again. Maybe this shared danger will remind us both what really matters.

"What do you think is going on?" I whisper.

"I don't know. But Damian is careful. They'll be back soon."

Finn and his simple logic. Finn and his supporting system. Finn and his impossible calm. *Finn*. I miss him.

"Could it be the Sliman? The ones we spotted near the library... they were getting close."

"Your guess is as good as mine, Tick."

"How long do we wait if they don't come back?"

Finn looks away but I don't need to see his face to know what he's thinking. After all this time, I can read him like a map. He doesn't want to think about the ominous possibility I've just voiced. He's already fighting the urge to run after Damian and Rabbit, to share the danger with them instead of sitting here, waiting. Finn doesn't sit still when there's something he can *do.*

It's his greatest strength—and his greatest weakness. He'd choose an adrenaline rush over safety any day. One of these times, that need for action will get him in real trouble.

"I won't think like that," he says after a long pause.

The forest grows darker with every passing minute. The trees stretch taller against the dimming sky. Shadows creep across the damp ground, long and shifting, as the moon begins its slow climb. Uncertainty presses down on us as the waiting stretches deep into the evening.

"Are you still mad at me?" The words tumble out before I can think them through. The surprise on Finn's face catches me off guard.

"Mad at you? I was never mad."

"You could've fooled me."

"Freya, don't you know me better than that? I wasn't mad. Maybe a bit disappointed, sure, but not mad. I felt you needed a break from me. It seems like you make the worst decisions when I'm around."

The ground beneath me grows warmer, and I reach over to ruffle his hair. "I don't know what I'd do without you."

"I know you don't."

I shove him playfully and tap his nose with two fingers.

He's about to retaliate when Daphne's sharp voice cuts through the moment. "Keep it down, Freya. We don't need the whole forest knowing we're here." She turns to Finn. "Can I talk to you?"

Finn nods and follows her a few steps away, far enough that I can't hear a thing. They take turns whispering into each other's ears. Whatever they're talking about doesn't seem to make either of them happy. Their expressions are tight, serious.

I feel a bit nauseous. I take a few deep breaths to control my growing anxiety. *What's going on?*

I should be glad about this, shouldn't I? Finn and Daphne finally getting along, trusting each other. We're supposed to be a team—the only free humans left on Earth, as far as we know. I should follow Finn's lead and extend an olive branch to Daphne. What is it that we really have to argue about anyway?

But the way she touches his arm when she leans in, the way he listens so closely—it bothers me, no matter how much I tell myself that it shouldn't. I don't have time to untangle these strange feelings. Is this how normal teenage girls felt when their older brother fell in love for the first time? When he drifted away from the things they used to do together—playing games, watching movies, or talking about comic books? When his world shifted, his focus narrowed, and he started living and breathing for someone else?

*What if Finn stops being Finn? What if he's already starting to?*

Theo's touchpad buzzes. Daphne springs next to him before the sound fades.

"What is it?" she says.

"It's Damian," Theo says. "They're on their way back."

Finally, some good news. Relief floods through me, washing away everything else—my jealousy, my confusion, all the tangled feelings about Finn and Daphne.

When Rabbit with his usual quicksilver grace and Damian with his solid frame emerge from the shadows, we close in around them, drawn by the gravity of the moment.

"It's bad," Damian says. "Whoever hit the camp was long gone by the time we got there. We never saw them."

"But that's good, right?" Tilly says. "Maybe it wasn't the Sliman. Maybe it was just wolves."

"Wolves don't take food and water supplies." Damian's tone leaves no room for argument. "Most of our stores are gone."

The silence lasts exactly one heartbeat before we all explode into words as fear and anger and confusion spill out.

Damian raises a hand. "Listen, we can't waste any more time. The camp isn't safe anymore. We need to find shelter for the night and rest while we can. Tomorrow, we figure out what's left and decide how to proceed."

Playtime is over, it seems. Time for some real growing up.

# Chapter 11

I CAN'T SLEEP. I took the first shift with Nya and Biscuit, guarding the cave's mouth. It was a quiet two-hour stretch. Nya didn't utter a single word and Biscuit was too hungry to form a coherent thought. Now Doc and Theo have taken our place, but my thoughts keep circling like trapped birds, pressing and squeezing against my skull.

It took us nearly an hour to reach the mountain, stumbling through the dark over uneven terrain. Rabbit had spotted the cave during one of his secret runs. No one mentions how reckless those solitary running sprees were, not even Damian. Maybe we're all past caring about the rules that kept us safe yesterday.

The cave stretches deep into the mountain's heart, large enough to shelter thirty people comfortably, maybe more. Cool air filters in through the entrance, and the floor is soft with moss. The walls feel smooth under my fingers except for the places where someone carved strange patterns with a sharp blade. I try not to think about who might have sheltered here before us, or why they left.

In the darkness, I squeeze my eyes shut and pretend we're inside a massive turtle shell, or maybe an egg waiting to hatch. We could survive here if we had to, hidden away from whatever raided our camp. A protective cocoon, keeping us safe.

Everything will be okay. That's what I keep telling myself.

✦

WHEN DAWN ARRIVES, I open my eyes to a splitting headache—maybe my brain's rebelling against one more sleepless night. What little rest I managed was plagued with nightmares of chaos, fire and destruction that refuse to fade even now.

I hear whispers and turn my head toward them. Two silhouettes are outlined against the rocky wall—Damian and Finn. Their hushed tones and tense postures suggest a heated discussion. I'm about to sit up when I notice a hand resting on my thigh. My eyes follow the line of the arm to find Tilly curled beside me. She must have moved closer during the night. Her face is so peaceful and innocent it almost breaks my heart. She reminds me of my baby sisters. I've grown to care for her the way I would have cared for them if we'd been given the chance to stay together.

I ease Tilly's hand away and make my way across the cave to Damian and Finn. They fall silent when they see me.

"Any news?" I ask.

Finn glances at me for a heartbeat, then looks away. "Scout and Rabbit are checking the camp." It doesn't take a mind reader to know he's not happy about it.

Before I can ask him what he thinks about the whole situation, two sharp voices slice through the quiet. I flinch. One of the voices belongs to Nya, who's always composed. In all our time together, I've never heard her raise her voice. The second one belongs to Zoe, usually the most level-headed among us. To make it worse, they're having a full-blown argument while on guard at the cave entrance.

"What the hell is happening to us?" I mutter, glancing at Finn and Damian.

"I'll handle it," Damian says, already moving toward the conflict.

I don't miss the way Finn's gaze lingers on Damian's back, hands clenched at his sides, before he turns to me. "This is what pressure does to people," he mutters under his breath. The edge in his voice makes me wonder if it's really Nya and Zoe he's talking about.

I brace myself for the inevitable explosion when Damian confronts them, but it never comes. Instead, *Red* surprises me. He takes both Zoe and Nya's hands, his voice calm, carrying just enough authority to make them listen.

"Hey, you need to keep your cool," he says. "Right now, we need our heads squarely on our shoulders more than ever. I know patience is hard when everything might be falling apart, but we can't let fear get to us. If we do, we risk losing everything we've worked so hard to biuld."

Zoe sighs, rubbing her temple. "I'm sorry. I don't know what came over me. You're right, Damian. This is stupid."

She reaches for Nya, who accepts the peace offering with a silent nod, and just like that, the storm passes.

Daphne springs up next to Zoe and pats her on the back. "Rough night, huh?" she says. "Get some rest. I'll take over."

I think I've seen it all when Finn volunteers to keep watch with Daphne and she accepts... *with a smile*. I shake my head to clear the intrusive thoughts. Enough with the Finn and Daphne stuff. The whole world is crumbling around us. I can't fixate on whatever relationship they might have like some character in those ancient teenage dramas.

I glance about the cave. Doc and Theo work on their touchpads. Tilly's awake and chatting with Biscuit. Zoe and Nya collapse in different corners, drifting into sleep land. Damian strides past the cave mouth where Finn and

Daphne stand watch, disappearing into the gray morning light.

I decide to follow him out. "Mind if I take a short walk?" I ask him.

"Why not?" He pauses for a second. Something shifts in his expression. "I think I'll join you."

His words throw me off balance, leaving me somewhere between disbelief and unease. It feels like I'm having a dream—good or bad, I'm not sure yet. Any other time, I'd have made an excuse to be alone, but there's something off about him today, something that makes me curious enough to let him come along.

The forest wraps around us, cool and damp with morning. We walk in silence until his voice breaks it. "Are you scared?"

"Scared?" I glance at him, caught off guard. "I haven't been scared since the day I came into this world, or maybe I've been scared the whole time. Not sure which."

He stops midstride, turning to look at me with a raised brow. "You say the strangest things sometimes, Freya."

"Well, you should know. You've been acting pretty strange yourself lately."

We keep walking. His hand reaches up to brush leaves and branches. I try not to think it, but I do. It looks good on him, this gentleness.

"Not strange," he says after a moment. "I'm scared."

The admission stops me cold in my tracks. *Damian.*

*Scared.* It's so out of character that I can't help but won-der if this is some kind of test. "Did you just say you're scared?" I whisper.

He turns to face me. His eyes catch the faint morning light, their blue startlingly deep against the shadows of the forest. I can't help the thought. Damian is handsome—or would be if he relaxed a little.

"You heard me," he says with a sigh. "We're getting so close to the end of our fairy tale. And it doesn't feel right. It doesn't feel fair that we'd go through all this, the escape, the hiding, living like fugitives, building something real, training for survival, and then one day, boom, all gone and we're back to plantation life, waiting for our turn to slip into the unknown."

"It's not..." I start to say but can't go on.

"It's not what?" he eggs me on.

"It's not like you to talk like this." There, I said it.

He snorts, shaking his head. "How would you know?"

"How would I know? Damian, everyone knows."

"Nobody knows anything, Freya. We pretend we know, but we're like puppets, thrown onto this planet as an ex-periment. We're empty shells filled with borrowed mem-ories, lost experiences and dreams of a world we never knew. We act as if we know what we're doing, but our plans may soon be spat out like poison."

"Wow," I say, trying to lighten his dark mood, "what have you been reading?"

Damian smiles, but his heart isn't in it. Now I'm really starting to feel scared. If *he* cracks under pressure, if our fierce leader loses his composure, we're in deeper trouble than I thought. For all his rough edges, he's the glue holding us together.

I grab his arm, forcing him to face me. "Why are you telling me all this?"

"Because you get it," he says, his gaze boring into mine. "I see it in your eyes, Freya. You can't hide it. You think like me, no matter how hard you try to convince yourself otherwise. You understand the hopelessness of all this."

We stand there, caught in each other's gaze. Something dangerous starts to build in the space between us. I want to argue, to tell him he's wrong, but the truth is, he's not. Before I can come up with a response, the light on his touchpad flashes, cutting through the moment like a lifeline. His vulnerability was becoming intoxicating.

"Rabbit," he says into the device. His voice is all business now. "What did you find?"

"Something you need to see. Bring everyone back to camp."

"Rabbit, I'm in no mood for games, just tell me what you've found."

"No way," Rabbit replies. "It won't be nearly as fun if I tell you. Trust me, you all need to see this. It's safe, I promise."

Damian unleashes a string of curses, already turning

back toward the cave. Just like that, he's forgotten about me and our shared moment of truth. The mask of leadership slides back into place like it never slipped.

I stand there, confused. I don't know if Damian was playing me or if, for a moment, he was being honest. I don't know whether I want to be his friend or slap him across the face.

Reluctantly, I trail after him. Part of me is glad he's back to acting like his usual brutish self. At least something in this chaotic world hasn't changed. But I will never forget what I saw beneath that rugged exterior. And whether he likes it or not, it'll be a lot harder for him to keep up the almighty act around me.

# Chapter 12

WE REACH THE HILL where Rabbit and Scout have been waiting. I brace myself, expecting something completely wild—shocking, really. Rabbit being secretive, let alone patient, can only mean trouble. This is the kid who once spoiled the surprise party he planned for Scout, because he couldn't contain his excitement for more than thirty seconds.

I crest the hill and take a look below at the sprawling forest and the concrete bulk of the facilities. The view steals my breath. I cannot believe what I'm seeing. I glance at the others. Their stunned expressions confirm I'm not dreaming. Tilly and Biscuit break our bewildered silence, doubling over with laughter.

Our camp has been overtaken by apes. Not Sliman guards, not alien raiders, not escaped humans. Not the apes from books at the library either, but massive, powerful beasts that move with an uncanny intelligence. The sight is so absurd that we can't help but crack a smile.

Except for Damian. His brows knit together as he stares at the apes. His hand tightens on his pulse gun. "How is this possible?"

That's my question too, but right now, I'm too transfixed by the impossible scene below to care about the answer.

Apes. Actual apes. They look like supersized chimpanzees, and they shouldn't be here. Our forests and mountains are nowhere near their natural habitat. These creatures don't belong. And yet, here they are.

Doc steps up beside Damian. "I remember something. Back at the lab in Plantation-4 when I was a trainee," he says. "This wasn't just rumor—it was real. There was a project, one of the more ambitious experiments. It involved altering chimpanzee DNA to make them more... human."

I turn back to study the scene below, seeing it with new eyes. Seven chimps, big, strong, agile. I watch closely as one of them gestures with its hands, and another responds with an equally deliberate motion. It's not random. It's purposeful.

*Communication.*

"They're using a form of sign language," I murmur, more to myself than anyone else.

One of the chimps delicately lifts a cup to its lips,

mimicking the way we drink. Another sits cross-legged on the ground, holding a touchpad in its large hands, turning it over as if trying to understand its purpose.

"Yeah, these are no ordinary apes," Theo says.

"Look at that," Damian says. His lips twist into a smile. "They're *aping* our behavior."

Damian just cracked a joke. We may be more shocked by that than the superintelligent primates invading our camp. Who *is* this guy and what has he done with our leader?

Finn leans forward, squinting. "How did they get here? Do you think they escaped?"

"Unlikely." Doc's voice has that clinical edge he gets when he's trying to explain important things. "More likely they were released into the wild. Set loose for whatever twisted purpose their creators had in mind."

"Creators?" Zoe spits out the word. "You mean tormentors."

"Same thing," Theo says.

Tilly watches as one of the chimps swings lazily from a branch. "They almost look... happy."

"That's not happiness," Finn says. "There's nothing happy about being altered, about being ripped from your natural environment, thrown into a world that was never meant for you."

Daphne catches his eye. "Are we still talking about the chimps?"

Finn just shrugs.

"We need a plan," Damian says. "They have to go. Our crops barely feed us as it is—we can't support seven more mouths."

Biscuit's stomach growls. "Speaking of food, I'd share what they're having right now," he says, reminding us that we haven't eaten since yesterday.

"First things first," Damian says. "First we deal with the intruders, then with our stomachs."

Theo heads for the HQ to activate the alarm siren while the rest of us ready our pulse guns. Doc swears they've been conditioned to fear weapons—something about their *training*. Between the guns, some shouting and the siren, they shouldn't stick around long.

"Good thing the Armory was locked," Rabbit says. "Can you imagine them with real firepower?"

"They look gentle and kind of friendly," Tilly says.

"They don't belong here." Daphne's words are drowned out by the sudden wail of the siren.

The plan works like a charm. The chimpanzees scatter, running out of the camp and into the forest. We watch until the last one disappears from sight. They might return now that they know about our food stores, but we'll be ready. Score one for human intelligence. It takes more than a few DNA tweaks to outthink us.

"Don't forget what we talked about," Damian says in a low voice as he brushes past me.

As if I could ever forget.

FINN DUCKS INTO MY tent and drops to the floor beside me. Our tents, set apart from the main camp, were spared the chimps' rampage. The ones in the main area weren't so lucky—most of them were shredded or flattened.

"What's up, Tick? Is everything okay?"

I nod even as I realize that nothing is okay. Damian's right, everything looms over us, unpredictable and threatening to swallow us. This is what happens when humanity is reduced to a handful of lost kids playing at survival.

"Come on." Finn pushes himself up. "They need help cleaning up the facilities, updating security. Work never ends, right?"

"Finn—" I say his name to stop him from leaving.

He pauses. "Yeah?"

"If they're doing that to chimps, messing with their DNA and then tossing them aside like trash, what do you think they do with us? The ones they remove from the plantations. What happens to them?"

Finn shakes his head. "Let's hope we never have to find out."

"You always do that."

"Do what?"

"Avoid the hard questions. You won't look directly at

what's been staring us in the face since the day we were born."

"What do you want from me, Freya?" he says with a sigh.

"I want honesty. I don't want you trying to shield me from everything. You don't have to protect me all the time. It's crazy, but I understand *Damian* better than you these days. You're right here next to me, but I can't reach you. I don't know what's going on in that head of yours."

"Freya... It feels like I can't do anything right with you anymore. This is who I am, and I remember a time when you liked that. But you're right, I'm not the same Finn. None of us are the same. We're all growing, changing. Stop fighting it so hard."

"I'm not fighting anything," I say, my voice raw. "I'm terrified."

Before Finn can respond, Rabbit and Scout appear at the entrance of the tent.

Rabbit shifts from foot to foot. "Can we come in?"

I wave them in, almost grateful for the interruption. "Finn and I were just heading out to help the others."

"Yeah, but first—" Rabbit exchanges a look with Scout. "There's something you should know."

"Spit it out, Rabbit." Finn's impatience is written all over his face.

"Scout's moving to the empty tent next to mine," he announces as if revealing a groundbreaking discovery.

Scout nods in agreement, chin lifted in determination.

"What, *now?*" Finn says.

"Perfect timing, actually," Scout says. "My tent is trashed and I've been thinking about moving for weeks."

"Did you run this by Damian?" I say.

Finn chuckles as he pushes to his feet. "Did *you* when you moved here?" He stalks out of the tent before I can respond.

Rabbit frowns. "What's eating him?"

I press my palms against my knees. "Your guess is as good as mine."

"So, about my tent," Scout says. "What do you think, Freya?"

"I think..." I try to choose my words carefully. "You should tell Damian before you do anything."

"You're right, it's the proper thing to do," she agrees.

The proper thing. As if anything in this world fits that description.

◆

I SENSE THE TENSION in the Armory before a single word is uttered. Damian stands on one side of the room, Daphne and Finn across from him, like opposing armies. No one looks happy. When Damian spots Rabbit, Scout and me at the door, he calls Scout over.

She looks insecure and gloomy as she shuffles forward.

"Daphne tells me you want to move in with Finn's group," Damian says. "Is that true?"

"Um, I guess."

"You guess or you know?"

"I guess... I know?"

Tilly snorts, trying to suppress a laugh, but it slips out. It does nothing to ease the tension; if anything, it makes it worse. For a moment, I hope the distraction will shift Damian's focus and *Red* will come out to snap at Tilly, and everything will go back to normal.

But then Daphne speaks. "Where people sleep should be their choice."

This is... new. Daphne's challenging Damian, her closest ally, her best friend, not to mention our group leader, in front of everyone.

It's so unexpected, it leaves even Damian looking stunned. He wavers for a moment, like he's trying to process the betrayal. "You have no say in this," he says, each word carefully controlled, though I can sense the storm brewing underneath.

Daphne doesn't back down. "I don't have a say. But Scout does."

"Enough. We have more urgent matters to deal with," Damian snaps.

That should have been the end of it, followed by a Daphne apology, but instead she glances at Finn, urging him to jump in.

"Daphne's right," Finn says. "You can't control our personal lives just because we chose you to lead us in battle. We didn't break free from the plantations just to submit to you over every little decision."

*What is happening right now?*

The words are wrong, the voice is wrong—everything about this is wrong. It's so wildly out of character my jaw drops to the floor. This isn't Finn. Finn stands for unity, avoids conflict and respects Damian's authority. Right?

What kind of hold does Daphne have over Finn? I cannot put my finger on it. The way she manipulated him into becoming her mouthpiece... Unless...

Unless it's not manipulation at all. Unless it's something worse. Has he fallen for her?

"Would you like to be the leader, Finn? Is that what this is?" Damian spits his words out like venom, slowly and deliberately.

"I'm not challenging you, Damian. I'm reminding you that we're free people now. You can't snap at everyone who—"

"Snap?" Red rises in Damian's cheeks. He whirls toward Daphne. "Is that what I do? Just snap at people for no reason?"

Daphne hesitates, clearly taken aback. For a second, it looks like she might deflect, but then she lowers her gaze and mumbles, "You just snapped at me."

"This has gone far enough," Zoe says. "We're all

stretched thin, blowing off steam, but we have to keep it together. The work's not going to do itself."

It's clear most of us agree, or maybe we just want the tension to stop.

"You're right, Zoe," Damian says. His eyes are fixed on Finn.

"I'm sorry," Scout says. "I didn't mean to cause such a stir. I'll stay where I am and fix my old tent."

Damian's expression softens. "Do whatever you want, Scout. None of this is your fault." He turns and marches out of the Armory.

I grab Finn's arm and drag him to the back of the room. He doesn't resist. "What the hell is the matter with you?" I hiss under my breath.

"Nothing's the matter with me. I have everything under control."

"That was under control? You're doing exactly what you've always told me not to do. All those lectures—*Don't question authority, Freya. Not in public, Freya. You're too impulsive, Freya.*"

My mocking impression doesn't amuse him. His eyes are distant, like he's preoccupied. "I don't expect you to understand," he offers, "but I need you to trust me."

"Then help me understand. Don't shut me out."

"I can't. It's not up to me."

"It's Daphne, isn't it? What does that girl have over you? Did she decide she's had enough of Damian and you're the next best thing?"

"Cut it out, Freya. You don't know what you're talking about."

"So enlighten me. I'm all ears."

He licks his lips, then shakes his head. "I can't. I promised not to say anything. For now."

"Is that what all your whispered conversations have been about? Promises?"

"Drop it, Tick. Please."

I know I'm pushing him too hard, but I need the truth. "You're keeping secrets from me, Finn. How am I supposed to trust you?"

"I know it's asking a lot." His eyes plead with me. "Just... let it go for now."

But I can't let it go, not yet. "I can't believe you're conspiring with Daphne of all people."

He seems to be genuinely perplexed. "What is it with you and Daphne? She's fiercely loyal to our cause and to everyone's wellbeing. We're all partners here, Freya."

"Some more than others apparently." I turn on my heel and storm out of the Armory.

*Fiercely loyal.* Huh. Ask Damian about her loyalty. And Finn? All his loyalty has shifted to Daphne, leaving me standing on the outside.

Maybe I should talk to Damian about all this, but then again, he's probably figured it out. He's just like me after all. *Yuck.* The thought feels like a punch to the gut. I'm like Damian not only in our shared sense of doom, but we're both newly alone in the world, having lost our best friends.

# Chapter 13

WE WAKE UP TO a pounding thunderstorm. The rain falls hard and heavy on the camp, creating a curtain of water that seems to blur the lines between the ground and the sky, muffling the sounds of the forest. It's a good thing we stayed up late last night, tidying up and fixing what the chimps destroyed. Roofs were patched, mattresses replaced, and supplies gathered. Biscuit and Tilly even ventured out to our crops and came back with baskets of vegetables, fruits and grains to restock the storeroom. These alien-modified superfoods require minimal effort to grow, thriving in almost any conditions, a rare and bittersweet gift from our oppressors.

We rush outside to gather the few items left exposed to the rain—cooking pots, weather-worn blankets, scattered tools. The rainwater is cool and refreshing against my skin. It hits my face and runs down my arms, drenching my hair and clothes. I don't mind. There's something invigorating about the storm, a promise in the air, an invisible layer of possibilities.

Inside the kitchen, Biscuit has prepared breakfast. Warm aromas and spices fill the space, mingling with the humming of idle chit-chat. Everyone's spirits are high; the first thunderstorm in months has brought new energy to the camp. Even Damian and Daphne seem more at ease with each other.

It's striking how little it takes to make us happy: a good meal, the song of a bird, the drumming of heavy rain on the roof. These simple things remind us of what we've lost but also what we fight for. We want so little, yet we need so much. We need more than a storm. We need a different world, one with a future.

I sit by the window, listening to the laughter and chatter with a smile on my face. Sometimes I try to count the generations between us and the last naturally born humans. Are we the third generation? Fourth maybe? We can't know for sure.

Doc once overheard the alien directors refer to themselves as *Lagerians*, but we prefer to keep them nameless, as if that could diminish their power over us. The bastards erased all traces of the invasion with the same ruthless precision they used to create their mutant army of Sliman fighters. The Sliman, terrifying in their strength and brutality, are a grim mockery of us, sometimes looking more human than we do. It's as though the Lagerians wanted to hold up a distorted mirror, reminding us that they control not only our present but our very humanity.

The invasion must have been lightning-quick and devastating, leaving no room for resistance, no time to prepare. Whoever lived through it didn't—or couldn't—leave anything behind. No warnings scrawled on walls, no notes hidden for future generations to find.

I've searched every inch of the library for answers, running my fingers along dusty shelves, pulling books from shadows, searching for even the smallest clue about how we lost everything: a forgotten scrap of paper, a hastily scribbled message, some breadcrumb of truth. But there's nothing. It's as if humanity simply ceased to exist one day, leaving only lab-born children behind.

We ended where Lagerian rule began.

It's as if they rewrote the world in their own image, erasing everything that didn't serve their purpose. And maybe that's the cruelest thing they've done, not the labs, the plantations or the enslavement, but the complete annihilation of what came before. They've stolen our very sense of who we are.

I remember a phrase I read in the library in a book of quotations: *"Those who don't remember history are doomed to repeat it."* The words send a chill down my spine.

I track Finn's movements across the room, trying not to

make it too obvious. Every gesture, every expression feels like a code I can't crack, a message written in a language I used to know but have somehow forgotten.

Something's off with Tilly too. She's unusually quiet and her eyes are fixed on her plate. I miss her usual morning jokes.

The storm has settled into a gentle drizzle outside. By the time breakfast winds down, Finn has already disappeared along with most of the Saviors, leaving just Tilly, Biscuit, Theo, and Zoe with me in the kitchen.

Tilly sits alone, staring down at her hands, while Biscuit helps me clear the tables. Theo and Zoe are hunched over their touchpads, punching buttons with urgency, as if their efforts could save the world one keystroke at a time.

"Everything good?" Biscuit asks Theo with a yawn.

Theo frowns, not looking up. "Not sure. I'm a little worried about the thunderstorm. It might've interfered with our comm system."

"We're satellite dependent," Zoe adds. "If the connection drops, it could take hours to re-establish the link."

They exchange a glance and excuse themselves to head for Theo's tech lair. Whatever the issue is, it's clearly urgent and needs more research.

Tilly hasn't moved or spoken yet. I move closer, concerned she might be feeling sick. "What's wrong, Tilly?"

She shrugs, but her quick glance at Biscuit tells me everything I need to know.

"Hey, Biscuit," I say, keeping it casual. "I have to take care of something real quick before I forget. Tilly's not feeling great. You think you could work some of your famous cheer magic?"

"Leave it to Biscuit to bring sunshine into a cloudy day," he says with a grin, grabbing a chair and sliding it closer to Tilly.

I head for the door, leaving them alone together. Whatever's going on with Tilly, I have a hunch Biscuit might be the key to coaxing it out of her.

Outside, Daphne spars with Nya and Scout in the combat ring. The storm has passed, but its traces linger: muddy soil, glistening leaves and the fresh, earthy scent that comes after heavy rain.

I settle onto the damp ground, ignoring the humidity seeping through my clothes, and watch them train, testing reflexes, flexibility and balance. They're beautiful in the crystal-clear aftermath of the storm, innocent like playful children yet unwavering like seasoned warriors.

Nya and Scout jump high, aiming for a rope dangling ten feet overhead. Their timing is off—bodies collide midleap, and they both crash to the muddy ground. They glance at each other, trying not to laugh.

"Up, you fools!" Daphne shouts. "This isn't a playground. Take your training seriously."

Scout starts to stammer an apology, but Nya moves fast, gripping Daphne's arm.

"Interesting," she says. "Weren't you just lecturing Damian yesterday about snapping at people? Yet here you are, being bitchy."

For a moment, Daphne looks stunned, but it's a very brief moment. "Get your hands off me, you freak. And don't you *dare* call me bitchy again!"

"Then stop acting like it," Nya says. Sweat gleams on her dark skin, but her breathing is steady, controlled.

Daphne wrenches her arm free with a snarl, spitting out words I don't understand.

Scout steps between them. "Stop it, Daphne. You're not in charge here. You can't treat us like this."

Scout's eyes find mine, pleading with me to step in before things escalate further. I know I should, but I can't bring myself to move. Our petty dramas are exhausting me.

Scout's eyes hold mine for a moment longer. I hate the look of disappointment in them. I start to get up when Daphne suddenly pounces and shoves me back down. She stands over me, angry. When I push myself up again, she steps closer and forces me back down.

"What are you doing?"

"I don't want to hear your voice," she says, but then I think I see tears welling in her eyes. *Tears.* Another impossible thing in a week full of them. "Forget it," she says, then spins on her heel and storms away.

I sit there for a moment before Zoe appears, offering her hand to help me up.

"What the hell was that?" I say as I rise.

Zoe considers me with a look of concern that makes me uncomfortable. "She didn't mean it, Freya. Don't tell Damian."

*What's going on?*

Nya and Scout escape to the simulation rooms. I wave off Zoe's hand when she reaches to help me pat mud off my clothes.

"Please, Zoe, I can handle this myself," I say.

She backs off slightly but doesn't leave. I eye her warily as I clean myself up. She's really freaking me out. She acts like I've been mortally wounded or like I might fall apart at any moment.

"Fine, I won't tell Damian or Finn or anyone. You know that," I say.

Zoe exhales, visibly relieved. "Thank you, she'll apologize eventually."

"I won't hold my breath," I say, trying not to roll my eyes.

"It's the pressure," Zoe says as if that explains everything. "Tension between her and Damian. It's... complicated."

"Don't take this the wrong way, but how do you get along with her so well? She's a constant headache."

For some reason, Zoe is touched by my simple question.

"Sometimes it's the people who push others away the hardest who most need love."

# Chapter 14

IT TAKES EVERYTHING I have to get through practice and my daily duties. There's a wild animal inside me, clawing to break free, and I can't keep her quiet for much longer. I need space. Time to think, to breathe, but it's impossible. There's always someone hovering, asking questions, needing help.

I've considered slipping away from the camp, just for a little while, but that would mean defying Damian's direct orders. He made it clear that I'm not allowed to go anywhere alone anymore. Not even with Finn.

"Freya?" I hear Biscuit's voice behind my back.

"Hey, Biscuit. Everything okay?"

"I need to talk to you. It's about Tilly."

We make our way to the kitchen, where we bump into Doc.

His fingers are sticky with honey. He quickly yanks his

hands behind his back, but it's too late. We've seen the evidence.

Biscuit grins. "It's okay, Doc. Everyone steals honey from the kitchen. Honestly, you're probably the last one to give in."

"I need it for an ointment," Doc mumbles, "but you're right, it's hard to resist the sweetness."

"You don't have to tell me."

Doc leaves, clearly eager to escape the banter. As soon as he's gone, Biscuit reaches into the pantry and pulls out the honey jar. He digs out a heaping spoonful and offers it to me.

For a moment, everything else fades away. The amber sweetness melts on my tongue and I close my eyes, savoring one of the few pure pleasures we have left.

Biscuit leans against the counter, watching me with a smile. "Honey makes everything better, doesn't it?"

I nod, licking the last of it from my lips. "For a second, yeah. But seconds don't last."

He grabs another spoon and digs into the honey jar with swift, determined movements. Before long, the jar is half-empty, and my patience is hanging by a thread.

"Biscuit," I say, exasperated. "Tilly. Remember? That's why we're here."

He licks the spoon. "But it's so good. Don't you think honey is just delicious?"

"Everything's delicious to you. Focus."

"Fine, fine." He sets the jar down with a dramatic sigh. "Remember when you asked me to cheer up Tilly?"

"Yeah, of course."

"Well, I tried. I gave it everything I had. Used all my best moves. The juice-dripping face, the starving face, the sad puppy face, even my charming face. Nothing worked. She just sat there, sighing and counting on her fingers. And then... then she said something really weird. Like, alien-invasion level weird."

I raise an eyebrow. "Wait, you have a charming face?"

Biscuit grins and reaches for the jar again.

"Biscuit!" I pull the jar away before he can grab it. "Come on, finish the story."

"What story?"

I roll my eyes. "Tell me what Tilly said, you honey thief!"

"I'm pulling your leg, I knew what you meant," he says with a wink.

Give me patience. "Well?"

"She said that the rain reminded her of something Daphne said to someone about a dream she had. Something about a flood."

"That's a lot of somethings," I say. "What did she mean?"

"That's just it. When I asked, she clammed up. But then she did something even stranger."

He makes a move toward the honey jar again but stops

when he sees my glare. "She patted me on the head," he says. "Three times. Like this: pat, pat, pat. As if I were a cat or something."

Cats. Back at the breeding village, entire armies of stray cats roamed the outskirts, surviving on scraps and whatever they could scavenge. I used to sit for hours, stroking their warm fur and listening to their soothing purrs.

Suddenly, I remember that I never asked Tilly about Finn and Daphne. I never confirmed if it was really Daphne that Finn was speaking to in private. There's something here, a thread connecting it all, but I can't quite grasp it. It's like trying to catch mist.

Sometimes it feels like everyone has gone mad. Or maybe it's just me.

THE MOMENT I STEP out of the kitchen, it hits me. Something's wrong. No, not wrong exactly. Different. Like the calm before the storm.

The Saviors are gathered in the combat ring, and Theo stands in the middle. Nya flexes her bowstring over and over, the quiet snap-snap-snap setting my nerves on edge. Rabbit bounces on his toes, burning off energy. Daphne's gaze is fixed on Zoe's touchpad screen. Finn and Damian are talking—actually talking, their body language surprisingly amicable.

Biscuit strides past me, reaching the combat ring seconds before I do. "What's going on?" he asks.

"Something that could change everything," Finn says. "Theo and Zoe intercepted an alien transmission by accident. A message about a ship that's landing in the plantation district three days from now."

I blink, shocked. "How did that happen?"

"Theo was reconfiguring the communication satellite hooks," Finn says, his voice quickening. "Zoe spotted an incoming message being transmitted to Plantation-4. They managed to block it just in time."

"What good does that do us?" Biscuit says, glancing between Finn and Theo.

"We're confident the message never reached its destination. The Director at Plantation-4 won't know the ship is coming, which means he won't send the Sliman escort the ship has requested for the landing site."

My mind reels, trying to process the enormity of what he's saying. "And you're sure about that?"

"We're sure," Zoe says. "Not only did we block the message, but we also have the ability to send a response back to the ship, posing as Plantation-4."

If they're right, this could be more than a rare opportunity—it could be a gamechanger.

"What kind of response?" Nya says.

"We send a message confirming the escort," Theo explains. "It reassures the aliens onboard everything's proceeding as planned and keeps them from suspecting any-thing."

"And you're positive it won't be traced back to us?" Damian says.

Theo nods. "The system won't know the difference."

"Without their Sliman guards, the aliens are vulnera-ble," Finn says. His voice has an edge I don't like one bit. "Especially at dawn. That's when we should strike."

"Strike?" I say in disbelief.

"Nothing has been decided," Damian says sharply. "This is all speculation. We can't be certain they didn't send a second message, one you didn't intercept, Theo, or that this whole thing isn't a trap."

"A trap?" Daphne says. "They don't even know we exist."

Damian eyes her like he's just noticed her presence. "And how do you know that, Daphne? How do you know there aren't more resistance groups out there that *we* don't know about? What if this is a trap for someone else and we stumble right into it?"

"We won't have an opportunity like this for a very long time," Daphne insists. "The ship will practically land in our backyard. It's our one chance to drive some fear into their hearts, to let them know that humanity is still fight-ing."

"That doesn't make it any less dangerous," Doc cuts in.

"Are we even ready yet?" Tilly asks. It's good to hear her speaking again.

"What do you think, Finn?" Daphne says. Her eyes seek his with uncomfortable familiarity.

Finn takes his time before he answers. "I think we can't keep hiding forever. Maybe it's time to make sense of this alliance—to prove what the Saviors can really do."

Damian swallows hard. "We're not ready," he says. "You know that."

"We shouldn't underestimate the element of surprise," Finn counters. "Even if they suspect something, they won't expect a sudden attack."

"You do realize what this means? We'd have to abandon everything." Damian gestures at the camp around us, our home and shelter. "For good. If we survive intact, we'll be on the run."

Finn's face hardens. His mind is made up, consequences be damned. I've seen that look on his face too many times to count. To him, this isn't just about strategy. It's about what kind of people we are, what kind of people we want to be. And whether we're ready to risk everything to find out.

"We should vote," Daphne says.

Damian nods without looking at her. The decision is too big for one person to make.

We type *yes* or *no* into our touchpads. The results feed directly to Zoe's screen. It feels like we're all holding our breaths while Doc counts the ballots.

"Nine votes for yes and three votes for no," he says, staring at his feet. "We're going to war."

The silence is absolute as his words sink in. We've been soldiers in a shadow war for years, but it's the first time someone has said it out loud.

"All right then," Damian says. His voice holds no bitterness, only resignation. "We do this right. We'll need an airtight plan and a foolproof escape route. We work around the clock—we've got three days to turn ourselves into an army." He turns to Theo. "Send the message to the ship. Make sure they believe everything is in place."

Doc stands still, clenching his fists. He must be one of the three who voted no, the other two being Damian and I. Something feels very wrong, but maybe that's just me—always worrying, always overthinking, always waiting for the other shoe to drop. Or maybe Damian's caution is rubbing off on me.

After a few tense moments, Damian lays out the basics of the plan in the Armory. It's rough, just enough to get us started immediately. We split into groups: Damian, Daphne, Finn, Zoe and Theo stay behind to work out the details while the rest of us tackle the practicalities—weapons prep, supply inventory, combat gear, training drills.

I wish I could talk to Finn. I want to pull him aside, to let his unwavering confidence wash away my doubts even if his words frustrate me sometimes. He can keep his secrets, act strange, play whatever games he wants. Nothing and no one can take his place. No matter what, he will always be my home, my family, and the place that I come from.

# Chapter 15

Finn sits beside me in the forest clearing, but his mind is somewhere else entirely. The fading light of early evening paints everything with soft grays. We don't have much time. Damian has called a late-night strategy session in the Armory after supper, but for now, I cling to this fleeting moment. I know Finn accepted my invitation to spend time together because of his guilt over whatever secrets he's keeping. I won't push him to confess. He wouldn't, anyway.

The trees look strange and menacing in the dying light. Shadows ripple and lengthen, stretching over the flapping wings of birds hurrying back to their nests. Little feet scurry across yellow leaves and twigs.

The world feels suspended between light and dark, preparing for the terrors and fairy tales of night.

When you bear the weight of saving an entire world,

you start to notice how it defines you—how the landscape becomes part of your emotional reality. The forest isn't just a place anymore; it's an extension of us, of everything we're fighting to protect.

I want to say these things to Finn, but I don't know how to put my thoughts into words. I don't know how to give sound to feelings this big without diminishing them. Some things refuse to be captured in language.

"I'm glad we're doing this," I say instead.

"You mean the attack?"

"No," I say, smiling at him. "This. Us. Taking a moment like we used to. Remember? It hasn't been that long."

"Ah, that. I'm glad, too. Being your trusted friend... it's always been a pleasure."

He's not my Finn anymore. He has aged these last few weeks. He's taller, broader, scruffier. His boyish charm has been replaced by the intensity and roughness of the man he is destined to become. He's achingly handsome, serious in a new way, but also vulnerable like all honest, unguarded people.

"You know I'd still be in the plantation, withering away, if it weren't for you," I say, trying to get a spark out of him. "Or worse, I might have disappeared during one of their midnight transfers, and no one would have cared."

"I would have cared," Finn says without hesitation. "But you'd have broken free eventually. It was only a matter of time. Though they might've released you themselves just to get rid of their most troublesome brat."

"Wow, don't hold anything back, Finn. Tell me how you *really* feel about me."

For the first time all day, he smiles. "I think you haven't even scratched the surface of what you could be, Freya."

I laugh despite myself. "You realize that's just a clever way of saying I'm no good now."

"Not so clever, it seems," Finn teases. "If *you* could see through it."

We smile at how mean that last bit was. For a moment, it's like old times.

"Do you honestly think this is a good idea? To give away our position, our home, everything, just to take out a handful of aliens?" His face closes off, but I press on. "There are so many more out there. Is it worth it?"

"We have to start from somewhere, Tick. This is a one-time opportunity to strike without Sliman intervention." He gets even more serious, more rigid than I've ever seen him. "Nothing stays the same forever. Kids become adults. Rulers become slaves. If we are truly the Saviors, then this is our path—fighting, living on the run, giving hope to others."

I shake my head. "I just don't see how twelve kids can change anything, Finn. They're an army."

"We twelve kids will not win alone. We must give out a call to others. Our legend must grow. If there are others and they hear what we've done, they'll know it's possible."

"Even if that means death?" I say, though I already know he won't answer directly.

"Tick, they are not as powerful as they want us to believe. If they were, they wouldn't need us. They wouldn't need to turn us into weapons. The invaders are intelligent, sure, but they aren't strong anymore. They rely on the Sliman, and they rely on us. Why? I don't know, but I think it's desperation. Why else would they give us such powers and knowledge? Have you seen what Tilly can do? Nya? Daphne? Rabbit? Have you seen Damian in action? There isn't a single Sliman who could stand against him."

"Not a single one, no, but what about a hundred of them?"

"Have some faith. The Sliman are controlled. They're nothing without their masters pulling their strings. That's our advantage. We cannot be controlled. We rebel. We rise. That's what they fear most. If we can make them realize humans will never stay down, that we will always rise and strike back, then we'll see their true desperation."

I shrug. "I don't have any special skills or powers."

"You're essential to the team, Freya, we can't work without you. And don't sell yourself short—you can do some incredible things. Maybe there's even more in you, hidden, waiting."

"Like what? Damian wouldn't agree with you. He's told me more times than I can count that I'm useless and dangerous."

"So now you care about what Damian thinks? Freya, no one makes it this far if they don't have something special burning inside them. You understand weakness better than anyone. You see things most people miss. It's not a small thing."

"But—"

Finn pulls me into a hug and presses a kiss on my forehead. This sudden tenderness catches me off guard. I feel my eyes getting warm and wet. I force the tears back. I don't want him to know that I'm scared, afraid, not of dying or being captured but of losing him.

"Listen," he whispers against my hair. "After the battle, we need to sit down and talk. There's a lot I need to tell you."

"Why not now?"

"It can wait. For now, we need to stay focused. It's nothing major, okay?"

I nod, but if there's one thing I've learned, it's that things left unsaid have a way of becoming everything.

We return to the camp just as supper is being served. Biscuit has outdone himself. The table is set like it's a holiday feast—apple pie and cherry pie, stuffed zucchini, fried tomatoes, fresh orange juice, and even a vegetable soufflé. Candles cast soft light over the room. The best tablecloth is spread across the table—even its edges are straightened with care.

"Did you see Nya hit that target from like a mile away

with her arrow?" Tilly says. I have her on one side and Scout on the other. Between the two of them, it's like I'm trapped in a cage with birds that won't stop chirping.

Nya rolls her eyes from across the table. "A mile? Really, Tilly?"

Scout leans forward, nearly knocking over her juice. "You could blow up the entire alien ship from miles away."

"She did a great job," Damian says. "I've never seen you be that accurate before, Nya. A hundred times out of a hundred. Impressive."

Daphne raises her glass, and we all follow. Nya blushes and lowers her head.

"Everyone has gone above and beyond today. We're ready," Damian says with a gleam of appreciation in his eyes.

I can't be sure he truly believes what he's saying, but his confidence spreads through the room like wildfire. It's his job to inspire us, to make us believe we're capable of the impossible. Tonight, he's succeeding.

We eat and laugh, but we have a long evening ahead. Every detail must be perfect, every move rehearsed until it's instinct. Each Savior needs to understand their role, their purpose, their worth.

Tomorrow we will face our greatest test, and though no witnesses will record our first true stand against the alien invaders, we must give it everything we have.

Deep down, in the dark bottom of every slave's soul, there is a light and a hope that a day will come like the one that now approaches for the Saviors.

# Chapter 16

THE VIEW FROM THE observatory tower is clear and quiet like an undisturbed crater on the moon. Nothing has stirred for the last hour while I'm keeping watch—no whisper of wind, no rustling of leaves, no crackling sounds on dried grass. The humid heat of the late afternoon weighs everything down, pressing the world into submission.

The day has been an exhausting grind of arguing, agreeing, disagreeing, planning and second-guessing. Just when we thought we'd nailed down every detail, a new doubt would arise, sparking a new round of heated debates. If it weren't for Damian's sheer force of will, along with his knack for commanding attention and shutting down dissent, we'd probably still be talking ourselves in circles.

It will be dark soon and we'll have to get whatever sleep

we can before our departure. My watch ends in less than an hour, and I'm counting the minutes until I can find Finn, hoping to steal a few moments with him before I turn in.

My touchpad vibrates softly and a message from Damian flashes on the screen: ***Armory. Five minutes.***

There's no mention of finding someone to cover my watch. Maybe he doesn't think it matters anymore.

The sixty-five steps down from the tower feel like an ominous countdown. Outside, I stop to take it all in: the buildings, the camp, the tents, the familiar shapes of the trees against the fading light. For two years, this place has been home, and it might be the last time I see it.

When I find Damian in the Armory, he's sitting alone at the long table. He punches out keystrokes on his touchpad, his left hand pressed to his forehead. There's something unsettling about the way he holds himself—like a coil about to snap.

I get a very strange feeling, as if a cold wind has blown into the room and made everything ice. Damian's strong, symmetrical features turn to stone. My own hands get heavy like marble, and there's a strange sensation inside my chest, as if my blood can sense something terrifying.

"Good, you're here," Damian says. His voice snaps me out of my weird trance. His face isn't made of stone and my hands aren't marble. I still have no idea why he'd want to talk to *me* of all people mere hours before the mission. Our relationship has been thorny more often than not. And while it feels like we might have reached some semblance of understanding the other day, private conversations aren't exactly our thing.

"Doc will join us soon," he says.

I feel like an idiot. Of course, this isn't a private discussion. Why did I assume otherwise? At the same time, I'm relieved and the icy feeling in my veins is completely gone. I cross the distance to the table and sink into the chair across from him, tucking my hair behind my ears. "What's this about? Is there a problem?"

"No, not really." The cold way he says it does little to reassure me. "I just want to inform you of a decision I've made that involves you."

"I'm all ears," I say, already dreading what's coming. If there's one thing I know about Damian, it's that he doesn't waste time with pleasantries.

For a moment, he hesitates. I can almost see him searching for the right words, an expression so rare on his face that it throws me completely off balance. Damian thrives on decisiveness. He lives to give orders, relishes the authority that comes with command. Hesitation is not part of his vocabulary.

"You know how things are," he says. "This will be our first real danger as a team since we came together. We've worked hard to come up with a plan—one that gives us the best chance of success. I've gone over it a million times, picked it apart and put it back together. And I've come to the conclusion that—"

He freezes mid-sentence, and my heart goes into panic mode. What if he thinks our plan is not viable? What if he calls it off on the eve of our journey? I don't think we would recover from this kind of disappointment. It would cast a shadow upon the camp that would be extremely hard to lift.

Damian's eyes flick to his blank screen, then he takes a slow sip of water like he's buying time. "I've decided that you won't be involved in the fight." He keeps avoiding my eyes as if he's trying to detach himself from his own words.

"What?"

"You're not ready, Freya, and I can't take a chance. You and Doc will stay in the back with the medical kit. If anyone gets hurt, you'll assist him. He'll guide you through it."

*Not ready. This again.* "You want me to play nurse? I'm a fighter, Damian." My hands are slick with sweat as a sharp heat rises in my chest. "I belong out there."

He meets my eyes now, brow creased. "You're impulsive, hot-headed, and you don't think clearly under pressure. How many times have you been shot, stabbed or run down during simulation?"

"That's simulation!" I snap. "You know I'm not afraid of combat or hardship. You know I'm part of this team."

"You are," he says firmly. "Which is why you will be

there, helping Doc. It's just as important as anything else. We need every link in the chain."

The iciness returns, and I go from feeling hot to feeling frozen within a split second. The room gets darker, closing in as if the walls are tightening around me. Damian looms larger, and I feel lightheaded.

"I want to be there with the rest of you, Damian. I want to help. What do I have to do to prove myself to you?" I say, but deep down I know it's too late. He'll never change his mind.

"This isn't personal, Freya. I'm not doing this to hurt you or upset you. It's the right thing to do. Doc needs someone he can count on and that someone is you. You'll stay out of trouble this time, and next time, you'll be ready. It's not the end of the world. There will be plenty more opportunities to kill and die."

It's impossible to tell if Damian is being sarcastic or dead sincere. My hands start to tremble. He notices and reaches across the table to take them in his. I jerk my hands away like they're on fire. I don't need his pity.

"I don't need to stay behind; I can protect myself. I don't need to be shielded from the dangers of battle," I say with quivering lips.

"It's not just you I'm shielding," he says, his tone so detached it cuts deeper than any insult. "It's also everyone else around you. We can't afford any accidents."

That's it then. This isn't about strategy or safety—it's

punishment. He's punishing me for every mistake I've made, for every time I've slipped up during training or refused to bow to his authority. For all the times I've challenged him, openly or otherwise, and failed to grovel enough. This is payback, and there's nothing I can do about it.

I think I might suffocate right in the middle of the Armory and that will be the end of my story. It's hard to breathe. My vision blurs. My instincts scream at me to run—to bolt from this room, dash through the camp, and vanish into the forest. But then the door opens and Doc strides in, and I know I can't do this to him. He has to stay behind, too, though I doubt Damian will crush him the same way.

Doc doesn't know yet. He greets us with a raised brow, clearly sensing the tension in the room, but Damian doesn't give him time to ask questions. Instead, he launches into the same speech he gave me about the importance of medical services, about how vital Doc's role will be to the mission.

But when Doc protests, there's no talk about him being a liability. Instead, Damian speaks of how invaluable Doc is, how we can't risk losing our only medic. Doc's talents make him irreplaceable; my flaws make me dangerous.

Doc accepts his fate with a nod. "I'll do my best to provide care and treatments for those who need it—now or in the future," he says, almost solemnly.

My fate is sealed along with his and I bite my tongue to avoid saying anything that might make him feel bad about me.

"Okay then, that's all for now," Damian says. "You two should coordinate your part of the mission before getting some rest. See you at midnight."

"Right, we won't let you down," Doc assures him.

I nod and follow Doc outside. The evening air feels like a weight pressing against my skin.

"I know you're disappointed," he says, taking my hand, "but we can't all be on the front lines."

"You're as good a fighter as anybody else, Doc. I've seen you in practice. You're skilled, patient, clear-headed. But you have to do what Damian wants you to do. He's in charge, right?" I realize that last remark came off as bitter but it's too late to take it back.

Doc shakes his head. "Do you want me to tell him I don't need help? That you should be allowed to fight?"

I reach out and squeeze his shoulder. "It wouldn't make a difference but thank you."

We reach Doc's tent and he invites me inside. I've always liked his space—it's neat, organized, and somehow comforting. Candlesticks are trimmed to perfection, test tubes are spotless, and his books are meticulously dusted.

Doc hands me a cup of water. "He's right, you know."

"Define right."

"We can't all be fighters. Not at the same time."

I FIND FINN IN his bed, studying the blueprints for the attack. What I see on his face resembles fear more than it does excitement or anticipation. Finn is anxious and I know it's not just about the fight.

"What's wrong?" he asks as soon as I throw myself into his chair.

"What makes you think something's wrong?"

"For starters, you're destroying your nails—your angry tell. Second, you look like you've been crying."

"I haven't been crying." I pause, examining my fingertips. "I *am* angry, I guess, so you're right about that part."

Finn sets down the blueprints and sits up. He's tired, he's nervous, clearly busy, I can see that. But I can't help myself. I relate everything that happened with Damian and Doc and the way I've been sidelined.

Finn takes hold of my hands to stop me from chewing my fingernails down to their roots. He listens patiently and waits for me to finish my story.

"He hates me," I conclude, kicking the small plastic table in front of me.

Finn sighs. "He doesn't hate you, Freya. He expects a lot from you."

"You weren't there when he claimed I'm a danger to everyone."

"Trust me, he doesn't hate you," he says again. "He just... well, he doesn't like anyone, not even himself."

"That last part I can understand."

Finn hesitates, glancing down at our joined hands. "Is it okay that I'm glad you'll be out of harm's way?"

"I can't believe you just said that. You're as bad as Damian," I say, although part of me is happy to hear him say it. I'm slowly beginning to accept the reality of the situation.

"Do you really believe that Damian hates you, Tick?" Finn says as I get up to go.

I sigh. "No, of course not. I honestly don't know why I let him get to me like that sometimes."

"Will you be okay?"

"I'll do what is expected of me. And, yes, I'll be okay with it."

Our entire future is at stake. My feelings right now are not that important.

❖

TWO HOURS LATER, I'm lying in bed with fitful premonitions racing through my mind. They keep me unhinged and alert, pulling me further and further from sleep. I hear the distant wallows of night birds, and then I hear the unnatural crackling of leaves. I quietly lean out of my tent and spot someone, Finn, tiptoeing slowly away from camp. He fades away into the dark oblivion of the primal forest.

# Chapter 17

THE SKY TURNS A blood orange as the sun begins its slow ascent over the surrounding mountains. After four grueling hours of marching through rough terrain and dense vegetation, we've finally emerged from the forest shadows into the mouth of the canyon. We are now crouched low on either side of the narrow pass, hiding behind shrubs, bushes and small trees. Doc and I are stationed at the very back as instructed. No matter what happens, we're to stay put.

The alien ship is expected to land in the canyon at any moment. We zigzagged our way here to avoid detection, careful to stay off obvious paths, though every snapped branch felt like a warning shot.

The pass connects the canyon to the only route leading to Plantation-4. It's just wide enough to accommodate the landing of a large ship. Once the aliens realize their

Sliman escort isn't coming, they'll have no choice but to move toward the pass on their own. Theo will ensure they can't reach out to the plantation for answers.

If we've learned anything from studying the alien leaders, it's that they don't waste time. Their arrogance is their weakness. In their minds, they have nothing to fear on a planet that's been stripped of free life. The Sliman escort is just a formality, a relic of procedure, not a necessity. To them, humanity is contained—they believe all humans have been rounded up and put in pens.

Theo and Zoe are also tasked with disabling the detection sensors around the closest plantations as soon as the ship lands. That's the plan, anyway. Whether it works as flawlessly in practice as it does in theory remains to be seen.

The plan itself hinges on precision and timing. Once the aliens reach the pass, we'll ambush them from all sides before they have a chance to react. If everything goes right, it could be over before they even know what hit them.

But that's a big *if*.

The invaders aren't the fearsome forces of legend anymore. The stories we heard from the older children painted a picture of something unstoppable. Now, after decades—a century maybe—on Earth, they've grown weaker. We've seen it in the plantations. Their reliance on the Sliman guards for physical strength, for any real exertion, has only deepened. They move slower, speak less, have even physically shrank.

But the why—the reason for their decline—is a mystery. We often joke that Earth itself is slowly erasing them.

We've observed their weaknesses closely, cataloging every vulnerability we can exploit. At dawn, they're at their most disoriented—a phenomenon we've dubbed their *blind spot*. Their vision falters, leaving them to rely heavily on auditory signals. It's a small window, but it's enough to give us the upper hand. If we can strike before they reach for their dreaded sensory receptor devices, we might stand a chance.

The receptor devices are a nightmare. They release powerful electric and magnetic fields capable of inflicting unbearable pain. The moment those devices come into play, the battle will tip in their favor. Our entire plan hinges on hitting them hard and fast, keeping them from even reaching for their weapons.

Finn suggested taking a prisoner, but Damian shot it down immediately. "Do that," he said, "and they'll hunt us down like animals. They'll raze the entire district if they think we've captured one of them. They won't hesitate to blow up the plantations themselves."

He's not wrong. They made this crystal clear at the plantations—if an alien was touched, even by accident, three children would vanish, taken away in the dead of night, never to return. The aliens wouldn't just retaliate; they'd annihilate. Capturing one of them would be seen as the ultimate challenge to their dominance, a provocation they wouldn't let stand.

Damian's strategy is simple and brutal: kill them all and vanish without a trace.

We'll cover our tracks meticulously, retreating to the mountains where we've prepared a small encampment. It's stocked with essentials—clothing, food, seeds—everything we need to start over. Again.

"We've started from scratch before, this won't be any different," Finn said this morning, but we all know that's not true.

Everything will be different. The Saviors will no longer be shadows in the dark, whispers of rebellion. By taking this stand, we'll be declaring war. The aliens will focus their attention and their wrath on us. They'll pour their resources into finding us, eradicating us. The world, already hostile and unforgiving, will become even more treacherous.

The sun climbs higher in the dim sky and there's still no sign of the alien ship. From where I'm positioned, I can't make out Damian's face, but I don't need to. His tension is evident in his shrugged shoulders and stiff neck.

My feelings for Damian are a tangled mess right now, like the sticky cookie batter Biscuit makes. I can sympathize with his pragmatic approach to our survival, his fears and the concerns he shared with me just days ago. Part of me even respects him for it, but his patronizing attitude still grates on my nerves, keeping me from fully warming to him.

Theo rubs his hands together before applying pressure on his temples. Zoe sits beside him, her hand moving in slow circles across his back, soothing his frayed nerves. Rabbit and Scout are restless—their legs and arms seem ready to spring up for fight-or-flight any moment now.

Across the pass, Nya, Tilly and Biscuit are distracting themselves with a quiet game of rock, paper, scissors.

Finn sits up front with Damian and Daphne. He's completely still, not a single muscle twitching on his flexible frame, as if his whole being is focused on something only he can see. Is it something to do with what he did last night?

I'm more at a loss now about his actions than I was when I saw him slip away into the darkness. He moved with the ease of a big cat among the shadows, leaping over fallen trunks like a ballet dancer.

My heart pounded and thundered wildly as I followed him into the unwelcoming grip of the night forest. I didn't think. I just acted. My instinct led me out of the tent and onto his trail as soon as his silhouette disappeared into the trees.

At first, I feared I'd lost him. I thought there was no point to my night chase, but as soon as I stepped into the forest, I heard his light footsteps on the dry soil and sensed the heaviness of his nervous breathing.

I slowed down when I caught sight of his back, making sure I maintained a safe distance. He didn't seem to sense me trailing him.

Finn stopped in front of an old, gigantic tree with roots like veins stretching out over the forest floor. I hid behind another tree a few feet away.

He knelt down on the earth and started digging with what I assumed was his knife. The blade moved methodically, slicing through the soil.

After a minute or two, he pulled something from his pocket and placed it in the hole he had just dug. From where I stood, I couldn't make out what the thing was exactly, but it was the size of an apple, perhaps some kind of box. A part of me expected Finn to suddenly look up, to catch me watching. But he never did. His mind was somewhere else, preoccupied with whatever secret he was burying.

The weight of secrets between us felt too heavy. If it weren't for the mission looming ahead, I might have stepped out from the shadows and confronted him right then and there. But I held myself back. Finn needed to stay strong and focused. If I unloaded my questions and fears onto him, I'd only distract him when he needed clarity the most.

So, I backed into the darkness and let him return to the camp.

The night got gloomier and more menacing when I was

left alone in the forest. When the sound of his footsteps faded completely, I approached the spot where he had hidden the box. It would have been easy—so easy—to dig up whatever he'd hidden. The soil was soft beneath my fingers.

But something stopped me.

I stood there, staring down at the dirt, realizing I didn't want to know.

*Not now. Not tonight.*

The thought of uncovering yet another secret, another potential betrayal, felt unbearable. Whatever Finn had buried, it was his to keep—for now.

I turned away. I didn't look back.

Now, perched inside a canyon, I wish I hadn't hesitated. I wish I knew what Finn is hiding. If I did, maybe I could focus on the present instead of being consumed by questions about a past I can't change or a future that may never come.

The sky shifts into a clear blue. The sun climbs higher on the horizon, spilling its rays over the canyon walls. With every passing moment, it becomes more and more clear that there won't be a landing today. The time has come and gone.

Frustration, anger and disillusionment bubble up inside me, a cocktail of emotions that words can't begin to describe. I glance at Theo who sits on a rock, his head hung low. He looks utterly defeated.

"I made a serious mistake," he says.

Zoe shakes her head. "No, that's not possible, Theo. I was there. I helped you decode the message. There's been no mistake, I can attest to that."

That leaves us with two unsettling possibilities: either the aliens changed their plans at the last minute, finding a new way to communicate with the plantation, or, far worse, they discovered their original message had been intercepted.

"Look at this," Finn says, crouching down to pick up something from the dirt. He holds up a small piece of thin flexible metal. It's unmistakably alien, crafted from the same material as the map I found in the forest.

"We have to get out of here," Damian whispers. "This could be a trap."

"If they knew we were here, they would have attacked us already," Daphne says, but she doesn't sound very convincing.

Damian's jaw tightens. "We're not taking any chances. Everyone, pack it up. Now."

We begin the strenuous trek back, retracing our steps through the dense forest. The path ahead stretches endlessly, another four hours of walking through rough terrain. Daphne walks in silence, her usual sharp tongue dulled by the morning's events. Finn lags behind the group, dwelling on who knows what, and I keep my distance, because I'm still upset about what I witnessed last night, and I don't want to make things worse.

Every minute that passes makes the day hotter. I keep my eyes on the ground, counting my steps. One word echoes in my mind, over and over: *trap*.

As strange as it sounds, with every step closer to the camp, a small part of me feels relieved. I was never fully convinced this mission was the right choice. Now we can retreat, regroup, and continue to grow stronger, sharpening our skills for the fight we'll eventually face. And I won't have to live with the fact that I was assigned to stay behind in the trenches while everyone else fought.

The sun climbs higher, scorching the forest floor and leaving us exposed. The way back feels longer, the trees offering little cover under the harsh light of midday.

By the time we're within five miles of the camp, it's just after noon. Damian raises a hand to signal a stop.

"Rabbit," he says. "Go out. Make sure the path is clear."

Rabbit takes off, his lean form disappearing into the trees. Scout and Biscuit exchange glances and step forward to take the lead. Between their sharp senses and instincts, it's unlikely anything could sneak up on us.

We slow our pace, giving Rabbit time to scout the area and report back. My thoughts drift back to Finn. How many times has he patrolled these parts, weaving through these trees? And how many times has he slipped away into the night, unseen and unheard?

Daphne looks even more tired and defeated than the

rest of us. And then I catch it—a brief exchange of glances between Finn and her.

A sudden rustle pulls my attention. Rabbit bursts through the trees, running at full speed. He stumbles as he reaches Damian, collapsing at his feet as he tries to halt his flight.

Damian takes a step back. "What is it?"

Rabbit clutches his knees, struggling to catch his breath.

Damian suddenly turns pale. He sees something in Rabbit's eyes that can only be described as terror.

# Chapter 18

"It's not chimps this time, is it?" Daphne says with a blank face that unnerves me more than Rabbit's wild-eyed panic.

Rabbit shakes his head.

"I knew something like this would happen." Daphne tilts her face to the unforgiving clear sky. She shuts her eyes, and I can't tell if it's to block out the scorching sun or if she's slipping into one of her psychic trances.

Damian stares at her like she's finally cracked, then herds us off the path and into the forest. His attention snaps back to Rabbit. "What did you see?"

"Sliman... they're everywhere... about three miles out." Rabbit gasps between shallow breaths. "They've cut off the northern approach to camp, sweeping through the forest like a plague. There's no way to get through them."

"Did they reach the camp?" Finn asks.

"I couldn't get close enough to be sure. But how could they have missed it? Once you're that close..."

Damian exhales hard. "We're turning back. We'll head for the mountains and reach the ridge by nightfall."

"We can't just run," Finn says. "Not without knowing. We need to confirm if the Sliman have found the camp, and if they know we've been using the abandoned facilities. We can't plan our next move based on guesses."

The veins in Damian's temples pulse. "And wasn't it your *last* brilliant idea that got us here in the first place? Attacking an alien ship against my command, walking straight into a trap. I warned you, but you had to have it your way. Isn't that why we're running now? Isn't that why we've lost the camp, our base? Isn't that why the Slimies are hunting us down as we speak?"

Boy, *he's pissed* doesn't begin to cover the rage rolling off him in waves.

"Turns out you guessed right, Damian, but on this we can't afford to guess. We have to circle around and approach the camp from the southern hills."

"And what would that accomplish exactly?" Damian says.

"From the hills, we'll have a vantage point. We'll be able to see what's going on in the camp without being seen. We'll know exactly what we're dealing with."

"Finn," Damian says, "I appreciate your dedication to the Saviors, your enthusiasm, your fierceness, your selflessness. I really do. But this is the most monumentally stupid idea you've come up with so far—even worse than trying to attack an alien ship."

"You know I'm right," Finn says as his features harden. "You can't protect us from danger anymore and you can't make this go away. My mistake, your mistake, it doesn't matter now. The danger is in our backyard. How long do you think it'll take them to pick up our tracks? We don't have time to cover them, and you know it. They'll find us no matter where we go. It's better to know what we're up against."

"I won't listen to this nonsense," Damian says. "We're leaving. Now."

For a moment, I think he might actually lose control and jump Finn. Instead, he swings his backpack over his shoulders with enough force to make the straps groan in protest. Theo and Doc exchange uncertain glances before quietly following his lead.

"Stop it," Daphne says. "Finn is right. It's too late to play it safe."

Damian's head whips toward her. At this point, I'm convinced Daphne would side with the Sliman just to contradict him. Something has fractured between the two of them, and it's anything but good.

"We don't have time for your embittered antics, Daphne," Damian snarls. "Pick up your stuff, we're heading to the encampment in the mountains."

"I'm staying right here with Finn," she says with a face as hard as stone. "We'll do this ourselves if we have to. We'll come and find you later."

I am so stunned my head spins. The unspoken conflict between Damian and Daphne has reached a boiling point. It's not just a difference of strategy—it's a rift splitting the Saviors in two. If this keeps escalating, we won't need the Sliman or the aliens to destroy us. We'll do their job for them.

"Finn didn't say he'd stay by himself," I protest. I look to him for support, but he doesn't return my glance. His gaze is locked on Daphne. When did I stop being able to read him? How did everything become so complicated?

"Finn is a big boy, Freya, you can't keep telling him what to do," Daphne says.

"Finn?" I'm desperate and I can't hide it.

"You're right, Freya," he says, "I didn't say I'd stay by myself, but as it turns out, I don't think I'll have to. Daphne's staying with me. Who else is with us?"

I think my head will explode any minute now as the pressure inside my skull gets unbearable. I turn to Damian, hoping for *something*—leadership, guidance, anything—but he pays no attention to me.

Everything happens at once.

Damian's entire being focuses in as he drops his backpack and, without warning, punches Finn square on the nose.

Finn staggers back, stunned for a fraction of a second, before he springs back up like a coiled wire snapping. His foot connects with Damian's stomach in a vicious kick.

Theo and Doc lunge forward to intervene, but they're no match for the sheer force and speed of Finn and Damian. They might as well try to stop a landslide.

"This is your doing," I hiss at Daphne. "Help me put an end to it!"

She nods, darting behind Damian with incredible speed. She grabs his right wrist and twists it behind his back. I don't have time to think. My fingers find the looped rope in my pocket. I whip it out, throw it over Finn's shoulders and tighten it before he can react. One sharp pull sends him crashing to the ground with a grunt of frustration.

I quickly throw myself over Finn, using my body as a shield against Damian's rage, who has already broken free from Daphne's stranglehold.

"Stop!" I scream. "Enough!"

Damian swears when he sees me, then stumbles as Daphne tackles his legs. He crashes down beside Finn and me. His breathing is hot and irregular in my ear. His face is bloody, his hair a tangled mess. He stares into my eyes for a long moment, then pushes himself up and reaches for his backpack.

Under me, Finn writhes in pain, and I'm grateful he has stopped fighting my rope, that he stays where he is.

"Let's go," Damian says, limping toward the path leading back to the mountains.

I ease myself off Finn and scan his injuries. His nose is bleeding and his lip is split, but I don't think anything's broken. "You will be fine," I tell him. "Come on. Let's go with Damian. It's over."

He shakes his head. "I'm not going anywhere, Tick," he whispers, using my nickname like a peace offering. "You go. I'll find you in the mountains after I see what's going on with my own eyes."

"Finn, I beg you," I say, my eyes welling with tears. I already know it's of no use. Once he makes up his mind, nothing can change it.

"I'll stay," Nya says with a flat, almost indifferent voice.

"Me, too," Rabbit says, shifting closer to Finn.

One by one, the younger Saviors line up beside Finn: Tilly, Scout, Biscuit. They all love him. Their loyalty to him is as unshakable as his stubbornness.

That leaves Theo, Zoe, Doc and me torn between the two sides, each of us wrestling with an impossible choice.

"I'm sorry," Theo says, "it's all my fault. I must've messed up when I linked to the satellite—maybe they noticed the messages I sent as Plantation-4. I don't know. All I know is something went wrong, and I can't let Damian down again."

We're too exhausted, too shocked to tell him what we're all thinking: that none of this is his fault, that his tech genius is the reason we've survived this long. Without him, we'd be fighting with stone-age weapons.

Doc sidles up next to Theo. His loyalty to Damian runs deeper than I realized. For better or worse, Damian is his anchor, and today's choice was probably the easiest for him.

Zoe hesitates, torn between her loyalty to Theo and Damian, and her friendship with Daphne—logic versus emotion. In the end, she follows Theo, aligning herself with Damian's group.

Now the four of them are staring at me and I don't know why I stay silent. I've known it all along: my decision isn't easy, but it was made the moment I first saw Finn, when something inside me clicked into place like a key finding its lock. So why can't I just say it? Why can't I put an end to the waiting and declare my loyalty to him?

Because deep down, I wish I could undo it all. I want to rewind time, to retrace my steps to the moment when Finn decided to defy Damian, to the moment he and Daphne started to get close. I want to make it all disappear like a bad dream. But that's not how this works. There's no going back. There's only the now.

So, I look at Damian and tell him that I'm sorry.

He shakes his head. "I hope I'll see you all soon," he says, "safe and sound, but I can't take part in this madness. I can't condone mutiny."

Doc steps to me and hands me a small tube of some

ointment. "For Finn," he says. "Apply it to the bruises and cuts every two to three hours. It will give him quick relief."

My heart breaks as I watch Damian lead Doc, Theo, and Zoe away, my chest aching with a storm of emotions. I know that Damian's right. Just as Finn was right when he told me that freedom comes with rules and responsibilities. But knowing doesn't make this any easier.

"Let's take a two-minute break," Finn says, breathlessly. "Then we'll head south."

He takes my hand and leads me to sit with him behind a massive oak tree, away from prying eyes. "You don't have to stay because of me," he whispers. "Do what you believe is right. You have to stay true to yourself, remember?"

"Bug off, Finn. Are you staying true to yourself right now? Is this what you're doing?" I take Doc's tube out of my pocket, unscrew the cap and dab some ointment onto his split lip, then rub it over the bruises on his cheek, perhaps a bit rougher than necessary. "Hold still," I mutter.

"It might not look that way, but yes, absolutely, that's what I'm doing," he says, wincing a little under my touch.

I pull him by the collar, yanking his face close to mine, and look straight into his green eyes. "What were you doing with that box last night?"

My question catches him unawares, and for a moment, he can't come up with anything to say. He stares at me puzzled and shocked at the same time.

"You followed me?" he says, his voice edged with disbelief.

"I was worried about you."

My words have somehow brought back the burden of that box. "Let it go," he says. "You don't have to follow me around and you don't need to know everything I do."

"Well, isn't that a joke?" I say, frustrated. "Everything? I barely know anything about the things you do anymore."

"You don't get to judge me," he snaps. "Do you think any of this is easy for me?"

"Do you want to know what I think, Finn? Honestly? I think you were wrong about attacking the ship and you're wrong about checking on the Sliman now. And both times you defied Damian just to be wrong."

"If that's what you think, why did you stay?" he says, irritated.

"Because you are everything to me and I can't live without you." I try to run off, but he is stronger than me. His hand closes around my wrist, forcing me back down beside him.

"Freya, it's going to be all right," he says softly. He closes me in his arms, pulling me against him, and places his lips on the tender spot between my cheek and my mouth. Instinctively, I turn my face and our lips touch. I feel the cut on his upper lip and the warmth of his bruised skin against mine. I feel like crying. We stay like this for what seems like an eternity until Daphne calls out his name.

"Finn! Where are you?"

He pulls back, resting his forehead against mine. "We should go," he whispers. "We're right here, Daphne!"

The magic is gone. My chest feels like it's collapsing in on itself.

Daphne shows up, looking tense and disheveled but composed. "We have to move." She takes a side glance at me. "Unless you've changed your mind."

"Finn is hurt," I say.

"I know, but there's nothing we can do about that right now. The others are getting restless and antsy. Finn, there's no time for breaks. Let's finish this and get the hell out of here."

Finn winces as he gets to his feet, pulling me up with him. "Gather everyone," he tells Daphne. "We're heading east before turning south."

The way to the camp is hard through uneven ground and thick vegetation, and we're exhausted. None of us have had proper rest in over twenty-four hours. We're frustrated and worried, but we keep moving, we keep checking our touchpad screens for signs of danger—sensors, cameras, monsters. We walk in silence and stay focused. We are companions, rebels, survivors. The Saviors. Broken, divided, but determined.

To approach the camp without being detected, we're forced to curve eastward, then southeast, circling around to come at it from the south.

I can't stop thinking about Damian, Theo, Zoe and Doc. I imagine them climbing the mountain trails, probably making better time than us. I hope we will reunite soon, hope that the rift between Damian and Finn can be mended and that the group can return to some semblance of harmony and rebuild what we lost.

Even as I think those things, my hope feels foolish. I'm not the type to believe in happy endings—instead, I see doom in everything, as Damian so aptly put it.

More than anything, I want Finn back. Not just physically—he's right here, yes, leading our ragged group through the undergrowth—but the Finn who used to spend hours with me in the library, who trained with me until we could barely stand, who laughed at my worst jokes.

He's hurting more than he lets on. I watch him favoring his right side, notice the slight hitch in his breathing, the stiffness of his movements. But he won't complain. He never does. I'm not sure he's even aware of his limitations. Even during the fight, he wouldn't yield to Damian, though we all know Damian's raw strength could crush a bear.

We reach the hills to the south after an exhausting climb. Finn points to the closest hill overlooking the camp, and we push through the last stretch to the summit. The view takes my breath away, for all the wrong reasons.

Five hundred feet below, the abandoned facilities are

swarming with Sliman. I count at least thirty of them, though I know there are likely more hidden inside the buildings or patrolling the forest.

Tilly gasps, pointing toward the Armory. "Two aliens. Directors."

I raise my binoculars and focus on the figures standing outside the Armory. Dressed in their signature black-and-red capes, the Directors give sharp, deliberate commands to the Sliman. Even from up here, their authority is undeniable. Each Plantation has five Directors, and these two appear to be overseeing every movement below.

Their faces are partially obscured by protective glasses. It's a necessity for them because Earth's sunlight progressively weakens their vision. The longer they stay on this planet, the more fragile they become. That's why they're rotated out at regular intervals with fresh replacements arriving to take over. Even the planet seems to reject them, wearing them down over time.

"We're dead meat," Biscuit whispers.

Rabbit scoffs. "If we're meat, we're already dead."

"Both of you, quiet," Tilly snaps. "I'm trying to listen."

Finn doesn't reprimand them. He's too focused on the activity below, like he's trying to will an answer into existence.

I lower my binoculars and glance at him. "Finn, we should go. We've seen enough."

We retreat down the slope until we're hidden from view. We all look to Finn with questioning eyes.

"We should fall back," Daphne says. "We could catch up with the others by nightfall."

Finn tightens his fists as if he's physically trying to hold back a decision he doesn't want to make.

"Daphne's right," I say. "This is too dangerous. We can't stay here."

Finn turns to Tilly. "Can you hear anything they're saying?"

Tilly frowns, straining to focus. Her brow furrows as she shakes her head. "No. It's just noise. Mumbled sounds. They're probably speaking their gibberish language. No one understands it, not even the Sliman."

"Try harder," Finn urges her. "If the Sliman don't understand gibberish, they'll eventually switch to our language. Any information we pick up could be vital."

Daphne folds her arms. "What exactly are you hoping to learn?"

"For starters, we need to figure out if this is a coincidence. Did they stumble on the camp by accident, or did they know exactly where to look? And what if they've upgraded their security systems? The satellites, the sensors—anything like that would be critical to know."

"What if there's a traitor among us?" Nya says, her expression as neutral as always, hands tight around her shock bow.

Finn considers her words but says nothing. He turns back to Tilly. "Is there any way you can catch some of what they're saying? You've managed from comparable distance before."

Tilly hesitates, her eyes darting nervously toward the ridge. "I... I can try, but it's all just noise right now. I can't focus."

"It's the stress that's interfering with your abilities," Daphne suggests. She steps forward, placing her hands firmly on Tilly's shoulders. Her voice softens, dropping to a hypnotic rhythm. "Tilly, look at me. Listen."

Tilly's gaze locks with Daphne's, and for the first time, I want Daphne's magic to work.

"You can do this, Tilly," Daphne says, her tone steady and unrelenting. "You can be who you want to be. You have extraordinary gifts. You can help us get out of this mess. We're counting on you."

Tilly blinks as if waking from a nap. She takes a deep breath. "I'll need to get closer," she says, and just like that her mind is made up.

I see the guilt on Finn's face as he assesses the situation. There's a terrible thought at the back of my mind I can't shake. What if Finn's stubbornness is connected to the box he hid in the forest? Why didn't I confront him last night? Why didn't I dig it up? Why didn't I tell Damian?

What if this entire mess could've been avoided if I'd acted differently?

I glance at him again. The guilt is still there, plain as day. Maybe I'm wrong about the box, maybe this is about the fight with Damian and his own lack of self-control. Or is it the pressure he's putting on Tilly when she's already so on edge?

Or... is it something else entirely?

"All right, Tilly," Finn says. "You'll need to get closer to the voices. I'll show you the safest way down the hillside. Are you absolutely sure you're ready for this?"

"Yes," Tilly says. "I want to try."

Finn crouches beside her. "This requires absolute precision. One wrong move, one snapped twig, and they'll spot you. You'll need to crawl down the slope, and you'll have to go very slow, very quiet, which can be tricky with all the loose soil and dead branches. The slope is steep, and you'll find yourself hanging by a thread at times. Are you certain?"

Tilly nods without hesitation. "I'm sure."

"How much closer do you think you need to get?"

"About a hundred feet, maybe. That should be enough."

"Okay, I know you can do this, Tilly."

"I'm going with her," Biscuit says. Concern has taken over his features.

Finn shakes his head. "No. Absolutely not. One person might slip past the Sliman and those sensory receptor devices, but two guarantees detection. It's suicide."

Tilly doesn't wait. She gets on her stomach and slowly crawls to the edge of the hilltop, inching forward like a shadow.

"The Sliman are moving in all directions," she whispers back to us. "They're clearing out our furniture and supplies. The Directors are supervising."

The rest of us crawl forward to the edge of the hill, craning our necks for a better view. It's unsettling to see the Plantation Directors out in the open—something they almost never do, especially in daylight. They move with eerie calm, gesturing to the Sliman, who carry out their commands with robotic precision. However they discovered the camp, it warranted this risk. They know about us now, and they won't rest until we're captured or eliminated.

Tilly crawls down another two feet, slower than a tortoise, calculating every movement before she makes it. Minutes stretch as we watch her navigate the treacherous slope, our heads hanging from the top of the hill.

She reaches a fallen pine tree trunk, long dead and sprawled across the ground. It's thick and sun-bleached, a natural barrier that blocks her view of the clearing below.

Tilly pauses, evaluating her options. She decides to go around the trunk and changes direction. Her progress is agonizingly slow, but she remains patient and determined. When her head reaches the edge of the trunk, she glances back at us, offering a brief, reassuring nod.

Then her sleeve catches on the rough bark.

Tilly tries to free herself, tugging gently, but the fabric refuses to budge. Growing impatient, she gives a sharper pull. The trunk shifts under the force, sliding a few inches forward.

For a moment, it stops.

Then, with a dreadful creak, the trunk begins to roll, gaining momentum on the steep slope. It tumbles faster and faster, carrying Tilly with it as her sleeve remains snagged on the edge.

"Tilly!" I whisper, panic rising in my throat.

Finn pinches my hand hard. "Hush."

I bite down on my lip to keep from crying out.

Tilly tumbles helplessly down the slope, the trunk dragging her along like a rag doll.

At last, by some miracle, she manages to tear herself free, sprawling into thick shrubbery. She lies completely still, hoping the thick bushes will hide her.

Slowly, carefully, she lifts her head just enough to peer through the leaves. She sees what we all see: a massive Sliman guard is scanning the hillside. His enhanced vision rakes over the shrubs where Tilly hides.

"Back away from the edge," Daphne urges us quietly. "We have to hide. Now."

We scramble backward on our hands and knees, too shocked to even feel scared or think about our diminishing options.

All of this becomes irrelevant when Biscuit takes a deep breath, crawls back to the edge of the cliff and starts down the slope after Tilly.

# Chapter 19

Finn told me once that a cool head and a warm heart is all you need to make it through life. Right now, I have neither. My head burns and my heart is cold as ice. I can't think. I can't move. I can barely process what's happening.

Finn and Daphne reach the edge of the hilltop in a second. I snap out of my stupor and follow them, with Scout and Rabbit close behind me.

Biscuit is on his belly, crawling closer to Tilly as fast as he can. Tilly's struggling to scramble back up toward him while two Sliman guards climb up the hillside.

"What now?" Daphne whispers.

"Just wait," Finn says. "We might be able to grab Biscuit and Tilly and run once they get closer. If not... we'll have to fight the two Sliman that are after them. If we take them out fast enough, we'll still have a chance to escape."

Tilly stands up suddenly. She looks at us with panic on her face and shouts: "I hear them now! The Directors know you're on the hilltop. They're ordering the Sliman to capture us all alive. Run! Just run!"

Finn turns ghostly white. Daphne retreats in shock.

"We have to run," she says. "The Saviors are too important to get caught like mice in a trap."

"Just how far do you think we'd get?" Finn whispers as he stands up.

"What are you saying? What do you want to do?"

Finn's eyes are fixed on the approaching Sliman. "There's only one option left. We surrender. At least that way, Damian and the others will have a chance to start over. They can rebuild the Saviors. We are lost, Daphne. That's it. End of game."

Scout lets out a sob. My heart sinks—everything around me feels distant and unreal.

Rabbit stands next to Finn. "I'm with you," he says. "I will do whatever you say."

"It wasn't supposed to end like this," Daphne whispers before she joins Finn and Rabbit, resigned to fate.

Finn looks at me, Scout and Nya. "I'm sorry about this mess," he says. "I'm sorry for all of this. Now let's go do this for our friends and for the future Saviors."

The finality of his words is crushing. I want to scream, to fight, to do *something*, but my body feels disconnected from my mind.

We start moving down the hill with our hands raised in surrender. The two Sliman guards below are closing in on Tilly and Biscuit who stay frozen in place.

With every step, the distance between us and the Sliman is shrinking.

I catch up to Finn. "Tell me you have a plan," I say.

"Sorry, Tick, no more aces up my sleeve. You were right about everything. I hope you can forgive me some day."

The two guards are only a few feet away from Tilly and Biscuit. Behind them, more Sliman are beginning to move in our direction. It will all be over soon. Our fate feels inevitable like a stone rolling downhill.

I look around and something doesn't feel right. "Finn, where's Nya?"

Finn turns his head back, scanning the hillside, and so do I. She's nowhere to be seen. Then, out of nowhere, Nya emerges on top of the hill, tall and majestic.

"There," Finn says, but I already see her. Even from this distance, I can see that her dark eyes have gone cold and steely, focused on a target below.

In one quick motion she raises her bow, pulls back the string and releases an explosive arrow into the heart of the Armory. There's a moment when nothing happens before the building explodes with a thunderous bang. Flames surge everywhere as a series of munitions ignite. Three injured Sliman stagger out of the inferno and collapse.

Before the alien Directors can react, Nya fires another arrow at the simulation building. The impact is immediate, and the structure erupts in flames. Next comes the headquarters, then the lab. The whole place goes up in roaring fireballs as smoke curls into the sky. Sliman guards scatter in confusion, a few converging outside the kitchen to shield the two stunned aliens with their massive bodies.

Finn and I look to each other stunned, terrified.

"What the hell has she done?" Daphne says.

Finn snaps back into action. "No point in surrendering now. They'll kill us. To the observatory tower!"

We take off at full speed down the hill. Biscuit and Tilly draw their pulse guns in unison and aim them at the two Sliman that are closing in on them.

"Finn," I shout, pointing at them.

A rough, guttural voice cuts across the sky making our skin crawl. "Catch them alive!"

The Sliman that remain standing, including the two who were closing in on Tilly and Biscuit, charge at us, guns in hand. I count fourteen of them and each one is a ferocious machine that knows no pain or fear.

We sprint toward the observatory, a narrow, three-story building with a single window on the third floor. It's isolated from the rest of the camp, standing a good hundred feet to the west. Over the years, we've used it as a lookout and have stored weapons and emergency supplies inside. Now, it's our only hope.

As we reach the building, we linger just long enough for Nya, Tilly and Biscuit to catch up. We enter the observatory just in time to slam the heavy steel door shut behind us before any of the Sliman can sneak in.

The staircase spirals tightly upward, so narrow only one person can go up at a time. Finn stops Nya as she starts to climb the stairs to get to the window. "How many arrows left?"

"Seven," she says. "One explosive, six regular." Her voice is steady, impermeable. It's no use trying to figure out why she did what she did, but I think the answer is simple, because for Nya things are always simple. She has been preparing for this moment all her life, silent and remote, perfecting her skills, working to achieve perfection at battle. For Nya, instinct is the compass, and surrender isn't in her vocabulary. She is the idealized version of our line of warriors.

"Make them count," Finn says as she moves up the stairs and takes her place at the lone window like a sniper lining up the shot that will decide the battle.

Daphne and Finn take their positions in front of the door, pulse guns in their hands. The rest of us fall into line behind them, bracing for the moment the Sliman break through the door.

Thick sweat drips down my eyebrows and my upper lip. My heart beats so hard I'm sure the Sliman can hear it. Tilly's right arm is bleeding. I rip a strip of fabric from my shirt and wrap it tightly around the wound.

Each blow reverberates through the walls, rattling the staircase. Then the banging suddenly stops.

The same hoarse voice as before speaks through a loudspeaker. "Surrender now and you will live. Keep resisting and you shall die. You have two minutes."

The nightmarish echo of those words spoken in the grotesque voice of an alien creature mimicking human speech is paralyzing.

My throat tightens. I can barely breathe.

"What are we going to do, Finn?" Rabbit says.

It's an impossible question and we know it. All eyes turn to Finn. His silence is the only answer we get. He's focused on the door as though his sheer will could hold it closed.

We exchange fleeting glances, quietly acknowledging how much we care for everyone in the room, how grateful we are to have known each other and to have dreamed of a better world together.

"I don't want to go back to the plantation," Scout says.

Finn lifts his gaze to the top of the staircase. "Nya, show time."

Nya nods from the railing, takes aim and fires her last explosive arrow at the two alien vehicles parked in the combat ring.

The arrow strikes with deadly accuracy. There's a deafening blast as flames and shrapnel erupt, consuming the parked vehicles and sending a shockwave through the camp.

Almost simultaneously the steel door is brought down, and the Sliman storm the observatory. Finn takes the first one down with a swift blow to the neck. Daphne sinks her knife deep in the thigh of the second Sliman, but they are both back on their feet seconds later.

More Sliman pour through the door, huge and expressionless like a night terror. It's clear they have orders to capture us, not kill us—at least not yet.

We refuse to go down without a fight even if it's hopeless. Maybe we'd stand a chance if Damian, Zoe, Theo and Doc were here, especially if the fight took place in the forest. We would be in our element then, using the terrain to our advantage, and we could make it nearly impossible for anyone to catch us.

We fight tooth and nail as the Sliman attack us with a singular purpose: to promptly disarm us and leave us defenseless. They know we're trapped—firing our pulse guns in this cramped space would be suicide anyway with our companions so close. Pulse guns can cause indiscriminate, irreparable damage. One blast could tear through friend and foe alike.

Nya comes down from the third floor, firing two arrows in rapid succession before a Sliman wrenches her bow away. Both arrows find their marks, sinking deep into Sliman chests. The remaining eight warriors roar in rage, probably because they underestimated us and didn't bother to thicken their skin to make it impenetrable. They didn't expect a real fight.

Two of them lunge for Nya, slamming her against the floor. Their boots connect with her back and head. Through my dimming vision, I see my friends falling one by one: Scout, dragged by her hair across the floor; Rabbit, face slick with blood; Tilly, stumbling, barely able to stand. Biscuit crashes to his knees as a Sliman boot presses against his back.

Even Daphne and Finn, our strongest fighters, can't hold out.

Daphne fights with the ferocity of a wild animal, her knife slicing through the air as she dodges and lunges. Finn moves like a panther, taking down one Sliman with a brutal kick to the knee before spinning to block another. But it's not enough. The Sliman overpower them both. Daphne's knife is torn from her hand, and Finn's arms are twisted behind his back.

I feel the deadly grip of a Sliman hand around my throat and realize what it feels like to have your life slowly squeezed out of you.

We are hauled outside and forced to our knees before the two aliens. They look exactly as I remember them from the plantation, though perhaps even more withered now. Despite their humanoid features, everything about them seems wrong—their hairless heads, their razor-wire voices, their nail-less fingers. They're small and frail, but their age is indeterminate and their true nature remains a mystery.

Their eyes dissect us as they whisper to each other, deciding our fate.

I find Scout's trembling hand beside me and grip it tight. She's shaking and I don't know what else I can do to soothe her. I scan the wreckage of what was once our home. The fires have died down, leaving nothing but charred walls, ashes and black soil. The only building standing is the kitchen. I can't hold back a bittersweet grin. One girl did all this. One human girl brought their plans crashing down.

One of the aliens reaches beneath his cape and withdraws a sensory receptor device. I've seen these things before, and almost always they were brought out during an emergency or for exhibition. Those devices are deceptively small, no larger than our own touchpads, but their power is terrifying.

They can levitate objects from a distance; they can generate powerful magnetic fields, produce huge amounts of energy, accelerate plant growth, illuminate entire Plantations, mend broken bones—or destroy everything in their path. But each use comes at a devastating cost to the aliens themselves, who share some mysterious physical connection with their technology. The more power they expend, the weaker they become, sometimes taking days to recover. It's why they use the devices sparingly, only when absolutely necessary.

The devices were used as a means of intimidation at the plantation, lifting us up and slamming us against walls. We soon learned there was nothing good to be expected when one of them was paraded in front of you.

The sensory receptors respond only to alien touch—not even the Sliman can control them. The aliens used to taunt us with that fact at Plantation-8. Finn and I were present when they practically threw one at us during inspection. A few children reached for it and tried to activate it. They ended up with scorched hands as the device defended itself, growing hot enough to burn.

The alien moves down our line, pressing the sensory receptor against each face in turn, starting with Biscuit, then Daphne, Nya, and Finn, while the second alien watches from a distance like a hawk.

My heart pounds harder with each scan, and when the device's cold surface finally touches my cheek, something inside me snaps. Before I can think, my hand shoots up and tears the receptor from the alien's grip.

I brace myself for the blow that will surely follow, but instead I see pure, undiluted fear in the alien's eyes. The sensory receptor buzzes to life in my palm as a red pulsing light beams out like a beacon.

Three Sliman lunge toward me, but I spring up to my feet fast, whirling the device at them. A moment later, they're airborne, suspended five feet off the ground before they're tossed with a thud against the walls behind them.

"Impossible," the second alien growls. I defiantly turn the device on him. He cowers and whimpers as I send a small electric field his way.

Finn overcomes his shock fast and, taking advantage of the confusion, springs to his feet with Daphne matching his fury stride for stride as they launch themselves at the Sliman guards. Their attack ignites the same determination in the others. Nya, Tilly, Scout, Rabbit, and Biscuit join the fray, transforming from prisoners to warriors in a heartbeat while I shoot electric blasts left and right.

A sharp ache shoots up my right hand that gets worse with each blast. The pain builds until it feels like my bones are splintering. I almost drop the receptor. I clutch it with both hands now, but it's like trying to hold lightning.

The power of the receptor weakens and becomes unstable. I'm losing control fast and the harder I try, the worse the outcome. I'm not the only one who takes notice of this. The Sliman notice, too.

*Of course they do.*

Two of them break away from the conflict with the Saviors and advance on me. I fire at them desperately, but my shots are pathetic sparks compared to the earlier wreckage. The receptor that felt like an extension of my hand refuses to obey anymore.

I take in the scene around me: my friends falling, one by

one, defeated. Their bodies are marked with fresh wounds as they're beaten back again and again. The only ones that are still putting up a decent fight are the two super-warriors, Daphne and Finn, but they are already faltering as they meet their limits against overwhelming odds.

My strength and concentration abandon me. I see the raised gun in the Sliman's hand and realize it's a tranquilizer. They don't want me dead. They want me alive to study me so they can dissect the mystery of how I controlled their precious receptor. They want to know how I'm doing what I'm doing. I almost laugh at the irony. I'd like to know that answer myself.

A second Sliman plunges at me with another tranq gun and then a third one. The receptor dies in my hands. Across the battlefield, Finn crumples under a barrage of blows. Daphne—our fierce, unstoppable Daphne—fights on, kicking, punching, keeps resisting like the fearless goddess that she is.

So, this is how it ends. It was good while it lasted. Our final stand, our last defiant breath.

The tranq guns align, aiming at my arms and legs. I close my eyes, getting ready for the blow. When I wake up from this, *if* I wake, I won't be me anymore.

"FREYA!"

A familiar voice screams out my name. My eyes snap open. I barely have a moment to watch Damian's face as he jumps on the nearest Sliman and breaks his neck with a single click. He leaps in front of me, gun in hand, ready to protect me with his own body.

Out of the ten Sliman left standing, eight close in on Damian. He throws his left arm behind his back and pushes me further away. The guns that are trained on him are not tranq guns. The first shot scratches his left shoulder. He fires back getting one more Sliman out of the way.

The second pulse blast rips into his thigh causing a deep gash. He stumbles for a moment but then rights himself and stands firm. My eyes get teary and my heart drops. All I can think is that I don't want him to die for me, that I'd give anything to protect him, to keep him safe. I'd give anything to go back in time and treat him with respect and appreciation for all that he has done for the Saviors. For all that he's doing for me now.

Out of the corner of my eye, I catch Theo, Zoe and Doc racing toward us, but they are too far away. They'll never reach us in time.

Damian hits one more Sliman before a shot tears through his right arm. I feel as if I've been struck myself. His gun drops, hitting the ground with an echo. He stands powerless as two more Sliman level their weapons at him.

No more games. No more warning shots. They are going for his chest.

The blasts are fired simultaneously, but Damian is left

standing. Daphne's freed herself and jumped in front of him. Her blonde hair falls onto her face as she stumbles backwards before collapsing.

Damian screams like a hurt animal. His voice rips through the air, raw and primal. The world fractures. Finn crawls to Daphne. Scout and Tilly stare in disbelief. Nya falls to her knees, pulling her hair. Rabbit presses his face into the scorched earth. Biscuit trembles uncontrollably. Zoe, Theo and Doc slow down as if suddenly frozen, unable to process this nightmare.

The Sliman don't bother with Damian anymore. He's broken, kneeling next to Daphne, his face streaked with grief and blood. The Sliman are coming for me.

*Their true prize.*

Something breaks inside me. A tremendous wave of rage and fury build up, flooding my veins, burning away fear, doubt, my humanity. I don't care about anything anymore. Not a single thing. My temples throb with each thundering heartbeat. I don't give a damn whether I live or die. My fists get tight around the receptor and only now do I realize I'm still holding it.

I yield its power with a fury and force I didn't think possible. The ground shakes when I target the two Sliman who shot Daphne. They fly up in the air and then sail backward like dolls in the wind and smash viciously against the burnt ruins.

I did that.

And more. I create a cyclone that sweeps everything upward in a hungry spiral—rocks, debris, weapons, branches, leaves. My fury is now directed at the two aliens. I march toward them with big strides. My features harden up to the point that I don't think they will ever return to normal. My hatred is overpowering, overwhelming. It's all that exists right now.

New vehicles approach, bringing reinforcements. Let them come. I can take them all on. I won't stop until they're all torn apart, little specks of dust on their way to oblivion. I will kick the whole bloody species back to whatever galaxy where they crawled from and watch them blow up into tiny pieces.

The receptor pulses in harmony with my thoughts, ready to reduce them all to stardust.

A new group of Sliman pour onto the battlefield, weapons raised, eyes fixed on me.

"Freeze them," I whisper, and the receptor spews out a curtain of ice. It's not enough to freeze them, but it becomes clear that the receptor isn't just responding to my touch; it's connected to my mind and will do whatever I want it to do.

I blow away the new wave of Sliman like leaves in a storm with a blue electromagnetic blast. They are taken aback, then switch tactics. Two Sliman take off towards my friends huddling around Daphne. One of them yanks Tilly's hair while the other kicks Rabbit in the shin. Their ploy works for them as my focus splits. Suddenly, four Sliman run towards me from different directions, and before I know it, four guns are pointed at me like compass points.

I order the receptor to blow them all up, but it's a confusing request and I have to refocus my attention. I spin, channeling power through motion. Their first shot misses me by a few inches. The spinning increases the power of the receptor to the point that I think I can set the whole forest on fire. A blue mist pours out of the receptor, covering me like a shield. Their next pulse blast dissolves against the mist, harmless.

The aliens bark orders to retreat. The Sliman drag Tilly with them as they back away. The aliens glare at me with a mixture of fear and calculation. They don't want me dead, but they don't want to die either. Their intention is clear: they will regroup and organize a manhunt designed especially for me. I'll be hunted for as long as the Lagerian species remains on this planet... until their last breath on Earth.

They release Tilly only when I raise the receptor one final time, then flee in their vehicles. I could probably blow them to pieces, but I feel completely drained.

I drop to my knees, overwhelmed by suspended emotions and physical exhaustion. When I look at my friends, my family, beaten, bloodied and heartbroken, my blood freezes.

The Saviors stare at me with caution as if I were a stranger.

# Chapter 20

DARKNESS HAS CREPT INSIDE the forest, turning the greens to browns and grays, causing pupils to dilate and hearts to shrink.

We've traveled as far as we can on our way to the mountains, but we can't go any further. We are bodies without spirit, legs without muscles, thoughts without hope.

Daphne lies on the ground. Her breathing is labored and forced. Her eyes are closed. Her connection to the world is fading.

Doc has tried to tend to her but there's nothing more he can do.

Zoe is inconsolable. She, Theo and Doc are the only ones that haven't been injured. They are alert enough to fully comprehend the weight of our situation. Zoe caresses Daphne's hair while trying to hold back her sobs.

Finn hasn't said a single word but I know he's in great

pain emotionally and physically. He has been badly hurt as are Tilly, Nya, Rabbit and, worst of all, Damian.

I am numb, confused, I can't make sense of anything.

"Freya," I hear my name whispered. I look up and see Zoe who wants me to go to her. Her face is pale but a glimmer of hope emerges on it.

"Daphne has asked for you," she says.

I am paralyzed. My body won't move.

"Go, Freya, talk to her," Zoe insists. "Your name has been on her lips since she regained consciousness."

I feel the anguish in Zoe's voice, but I can't talk. I can't form a single sensible sentence. I want to tell Daphne that I'm sorry, but what good is that now? I'm sorry for all my petty thoughts. I'm sorry for my jealousy. I'm sorry for my arrogance. I'm sorry I made you my enemy.

I don't know how to say any of this, so I kneel next to her silently. Daphne moves her lips but no sound comes out. I lean over her. "I will make them pay, Daphne, I promise. No matter what it takes, I will destroy them all."

I tighten my fists around the alien device and squeeze it hard. It releases a rainbow of light that grows larger and larger until it encompasses the trees all around us. The forest is lit with colors and shimmering lines of energy. A little circle of yellow and white light sparks out of the receptor and lands on Daphne's face.

She opens her eyes with  a sudden burst of energy. She gazes at my face  and Zoe's face,  then stares at the suspended light with a smile on her lips.

"The flood of light. It was you," she says. "You were the one in my dream. You are the flood of light."

The smile lingers on her lips even as she leaves this world. The light around her turns into a white mist and it sprinkles down onto her.

The tears we have been holding back are free to roll down our cheeks. One by one we lean over Daphne to say goodbye. When it's Damian's turn, he hurries to walk away, hunched over and dragging his injured leg.

I walk over to Finn. I sit next to him and rest my head on his shoulder. The familiarity of this gesture seems strangely odd in the semi-darkness of the forest under the moonlight.

"Everything is my fault," he says. "I don't know what I was thinking, or maybe I simply wasn't thinking at all. I put all this in motion."

"No, if it's anyone's fault, it's mine, Finn. Daphne died because of the mess I got myself into, because I grabbed the sensory receptor from the alien, because I put Damian in a position where he had no option but to try to protect me."

"We shouldn't even be there," Finn says. "I shouldn't have convinced all those kids to go with me. We weren't ready. Damian knew it."

I know that he believes what he says. I know that he's overcome with guilt. I know that he's in pain. I'm not mad at him, not anymore—nobody can predict the future, why should he?

"It's no use blaming yourself. You had no idea this was going to happen. You followed your instincts. Now we have to regroup and move on. They know about us."

Finn looks at me with curiosity. "They know about you, you mean. They will not rest until they get their hands on you."

"Don't look at me like that," I beg of him.

"You connected with the receptor," he says. "You shouldn't have, but you did. You made the impossible happen. You connected to it more efficiently than the aliens themselves. Maybe Theo will have an explanation."

"You don't sound too surprised."

"I've always known you were special," he says with a wink. "How many times have I told you?"

"What are we going to do, Finn?"

"I'm the wrong guy to ask. Damian is our leader."

We don't say anything for a while. We will say goodbye to this forest that has been our home for so long. Daphne will never leave this place and we may never return. I will take her energy with me. I feel this more than I think it.

"What are you thinking?" Finn says.

"Daphne. Did you fall in love with her?"

He gives no response for what seems like an eternity.

"It doesn't matter," I say. "She's inside me now. I feel her. She'll always be with me."

Finn gives me a sad smile. "Silly, Tick. Daphne loved Damian for years. He didn't share her feelings, or maybe he didn't want to have feelings for anyone while he was responsible for our lives. Daphne tried to get him to change his mind, but he pushed her away. He became cold, distant. He stopped talking to her in private. He kept her at arm's length."

"But why did she confide in you? Does it have to do with the hidden box? Please, Finn, tell me."

He sighs as he turns his face away. "I need time to put everything in order inside my head. Daphne had a premonition that she was going to die in a flood. She didn't talk about her premonitions much, but she had quite a few that turned out to be fairly accurate according to her."

I remember now. She said I was in her dream. She called me the flood.

"She wanted to have some time with Damian before that happened," Finn continues. "She thought that if Damian temporarily lost his position as leader of the group, he might be more open to her. She asked for my help. She wanted me to find a way to challenge Damian. I didn't fully agree to that, but I did agree to show more initiative and put Damian in situations that would give her the opportunity to approach him when he was vulnerable. I made a terrible mistake."

"I want to know about the box," I tell him. "It consumes me."

"The box was Daphne's. She wanted me to give it to Damian after she was gone. I knew she was serious about this. I couldn't turn her down even though I never believed she was going to die, Freya, honest."

The trees bristle in the breeze unaware of our human struggles. I squeeze his hand. His burden weighs heavily on him. I want to help him carry it.

"Somebody should go find Damian," Finn says. "He's hurt in more ways than he will ever admit."

This is what I can do for Finn. Help Damian. "It's the least I can do," I say. "He saved my life even though all I've ever done is defy him."

"Thank him for all of us. He has always cared only about our wellbeing."

"Finn, we will get through this."

I let go of his hand and turn my eyes to the spot where Daphne's body lies, surrounded by the familiar faces of her friends and companions.

"Safe travels, Daphne," I whisper.

DAMIAN SITS AT THE root of a big oak tree. The sensory receptor casts a narrow beam of light like a flashlight. I can see him clearly. He is perfectly still, staring into the void of night. His arm and leg are clumsily bandaged. The bruises on his face have spread like dark shadows, yet he looks impossibly handsome, more striking than ever.

"Go away," he says without bothering to look at me.

I don't go. I sit by him. The look on his face is murderous when he turns it on me.

"Are you deaf?" He spews the words out slowly, putting emphasis on the *deaf* part, but then he starts laughing. His laughter fills the space around us with an angry intensity. It ricochets off the trees. It bounces off the ground and hurts my eardrums.

I fear he has gone mad.

"Fine, if you don't go, I will," he says as he stands up.

"It's not your fault," I say, but I don't think he cares. I get up and stand in front of him. "Daphne made the choice to give up her life for you. I know how terrible it feels, because in a way, she gave up her life for me, too." My voice breaks into a thousand tiny glass shards as I speak.

"What do you know?" Damian shouts at me. "You have no idea, so spare me your pity. You are clueless still even if you somehow turned into a superhero today. Now clear off and leave me alone."

"I'm not afraid of you," I say, trying to sound as calm as possible.

"Well, maybe you should be."

"I know a lot more than you think. I know Daphne loved you."

"Just shut up, Freya."

"I don't know when you realized that you loved her,

too. I don't know if it just hit you today or a long time ago." I grab his wrists as he tries to raise his hands to push me away. "She chose to jump in front of you because she loved you. It was her choice, her right."

"If she had just listened to me," he says as he begins fighting the pain in his heart, "I could have kept her safe."

"We will never be safe, Damian. We are fugitives. We are the Saviors. A lot of us will die and when more join us, they will die, too. Fewer will die with you leading us. You can't wallow in guilt. We all need you."

He remains silent but I can feel a pressure he doesn't understand building up in his chest, choking him, making him lightheaded.

"I came here to thank you," I tell him. "For saving me, for all that you did." I realize then that this is not what I came to say. This is what Finn wants me to say. My words would be questions, petty and confused and accusing him. I'd ask him why he came back for us. I'd ask why he didn't run to safety, to the mountains, when he had the chance.

He turns his face away. "I cared for Daphne. I respected and admired her, but you were wrong before. I didn't love her. Not the way she wanted."

I take a step backward when he moves toward me and locks his eyes on mine. Then another step and another until I find my back against a tree.

"Do you realize what you did back there, Freya?" he

says as he crouches down to level his eyes with mine. "You've changed the rules of the game forever. You are our future."

He kisses me and I want to fight him off but I don't. I stay in the kiss and when he gets his arms around me, I do the same. I don't know what I'm doing or why. I don't know why it feels good. Our pain swims away into the forest and the sun erupts into our hungry hearts. I wait for the guilt to begin but there are only his lips now.

My senses suddenly target a rustling among the trees. Finn. I turn my eyes and see his face stunned in the moonlight, watching us.

What have I done?

I push Damian away as I watch Finn disappear into the darkness.

"I'm sorry," Damian says. "That was stupid. I'm not myself."

"It's okay," I say as I set off running into the dark to catch up with Finn.

❖

I FIND THE OTHERS where I left them, but their focus has shifted. All eyes are on me now, including Finn's. I go red all the way to my ears. Has he told them what he just saw? The thought makes me want to disappear.

But it's not that. What I see in their eyes when I step

closer is not judgement. It's a flicker of hope, a flash of wonder.

"What's going on?" I say.

"We've been talking about you and the sensory receptor," Theo says. "It somehow synchronized with your brainwaves and nerve receptors and it responded to your touch. I have no explanation as to why it happened, but we all agree that you give us a fighting chance."

Theo hugs me and I hug him back, lost for words. "Can I hold it?" he asks.

I hand the receptor to him, and he presses a red button, then a yellow one. He closes his eyes, gives the receptor a little shake, but nothing happens.

"Just as I thought," he says. "You're the only one it likes."

Tilly bounces with barely contained excitement. "Who knows what else you'll be able to do with it."

"I'm pretty sure flying's not on the list, Tilly," I joke, stealing a glance at Finn.

His expression gives nothing away, but I feel like I have to explain myself. I want to tell him that what he saw wasn't real. It wasn't planned. It was a moment of weakness born of shock and pain and the heaviness of the day.

I want to tell him that my only commitment is to the Saviors and trying to figure out this unexpected connection to the receptor.

But why do I feel the need to redeem myself in his

eyes? Finn and I are friends. We're free to make our own choices. We've earned that right the hard way.

Rabbit, Scout, Tilly and Biscuit rush forward and wrap me in a group hug. Doc and Zoe exchange grins and flash the sign of victory. Even Nya offers me a subtle bow of respect.

Damian walks back to us and, to my surprise, shakes Finn's hand, as the energy in the group changes from dark to light. It hits me that this new chapter we're entering comes with a great deal more responsibility for me.

I will fight and I will persevere. I will set aside arrogance and self-pity. I will inspire those still in chains and I will protect the Saviors with my last breath. I will cherish every beat of their hearts.

And I will become a flood of light in the darkness.

# Chapter 21

THE LANDSCAPE CHANGES SLOWLY as we move north toward the mountains. The land becomes dryer, the trees shorter. The march is slow as we're injured and have to pause frequently to cover up our tracks and make sure we're not being followed.

Theo says he doesn't think the aliens will try to follow us, not while I'm in possession of the sensory receptor device, not while they have no understanding of what I can do with it. They will need to gather forces and devise a plan.

We'll have to live like nomads for a while until we find a new place to settle down, a place far away from the plantations.

At the break of dawn, we buried Daphne in the woods. We set off through the underground tunnel with heavy hearts. Now that we walk out in the sunshine again, with the heat burning our wounds and scorching our pride, I visualize Daphne's face one last time—her beautiful eyes, her proud gait and her intensity when she used the powers of her mind. I'm coming to terms with what has happened to her and with what lies ahead for me.

I will never forget her or my promise. I will find a way to avenge her death and the deaths of so many before her. We will find the strength to believe in each other again, and from now on I will not let doubt and fear dictate my actions.

It was no accident we all found our way to the Saviors. We were all meant to be here, and even I have discovered my role. I'm needed as much as anybody else, but, most importantly, we are not alone.

It's not just Finn and me anymore. Tilly, Rabbit, Theo, Zoe, Biscuit, Nya, Doc, Scout and Damian have become my family. Daphne will be remembered in my heart along with my sisters and brother and my poor, fractured mother.

Rabbit and Scout who have been leading the way signal for us to halt.

"There's someone out there," Rabbit says.

"About two hundred clicks ahead, hiding in the woods," Scout adds.

"Someone? What do you mean? Is it alien or Sliman?" Damian says.

"Human," Rabbit says. "It's human."

Tilly steps in and squints, trying to improve her focus. "If it's human, it's a small one. A child."

We move closer until we distinguish the small silhouette that lingers uncertainly in the distance.

"Rabbit, go get it or go kill it," Damian says.

Rabbit dashes off, leaving a cloud of dust flying up behind him. Our breathing slows down as we watch the scene. Rabbit covers the distance within seconds and grabs the child from behind. The child's limbs kick wildly in a desperate attempt to break free.

As Rabbit walks back toward us, holding the child in his arms, I feel a strange twinge in my heart. I know it's impossible, yet I recognize her right away. I've often thought of her, dreamed of one day seeing her, even chose a name for her.

She's very small and looks hungry. Her hair is short. Her eyes study each and every one of us. She's confused but not scared. She stretches her neck to show she has no fear of us.

"Let her go, Rabbit," I say, dryly.

Rabbit looks to Damian for approval. Damian nods that it's okay. Rabbit releases the girl and she stays right where she stands. I walk to her cautiously.

She considers me without any hesitation or doubt. Her tiny body straightens up in an attempt to appear taller. She lifts her hand to pat her hair down and then she wipes her hand on her brown uniform. On it, sewn with red and black thread, I see the insignia for Plantation-15.

I place my hands on her shoulders for a moment, then change my mind and put them on her red cheeks, closing her face inside them. My chest fills with tenderness and affection.

"Pip," I say. "Welcome to the Saviors."

# About the Author

Stella Fitzsimons was born in Athens, Greece, and lives in Southern California with her husband and two sons. After studying economics and language arts she went on to teach both Mathematics and English before launching *Stella's Literary Bistro*, a bilingual literary journal. Her works include: *Forest Runners, The Dark Legion, The Shadow Empire, Beyond the River of Time, The Vanishing Tome, Luna, Winter, Silver Dust, Shadow Fall, Moonlight Mist* and *The Last Rider.*